THE WHISTLE STOP MYSTERY

by Marjory Hall
illustrated by Mimi Korach

When twelve-year-old Barry Loomis learns that two big new highways are to meet in her small town of Northville, she isn't nearly as impressed as everyone else seems to be. Her cousin Alicia, who lives in the city, calls Northville a "whistle stop," and Barry is sure new roads won't be enough to change Alicia's negative opinion.

Soon, however, it appears that the new highways may make a difference. Because of them, the townspeople are suddenly talking furtively about the gloomy old Parrish mansion. And, almost overnight, many new people come to Northville: young Chris Clark, who seems shy and aloof; handsome Mr. Kenyon; Roy Upton, a sullen teen-ager; Ellen Conway, the new waitress at Millie's restaurant. Barry overhears her parents' worried conversation about the possible revival of Northville's "old trouble," but when she queries them about it, they refuse to give her any details.

Then Alicia comes for her annual summer visit, and Barry persuades her to join forces in finding out what is going on. Together, the girls succeed in convincing Chris to take part in their secret sleuthing. It is only after the young people become involved in a dangerous situation that they find out what is really happening in Northville. And then Alicia admits that it is "a wonderful, exciting, marvelous whistle stop!"

THE WHISTLE STOP MYSTERY

The

Whistle Stop Mystery

By MARJORY HALL

Illustrated by Mimi Korach

FUNK & WAGNALLS

NEW YORK

1

Other books by the same author

For Younger Readers

    MYSTERY AT LIONS GATE

For Teen-Age Readers

    LOOK AT ME!

    CLOTHESHORSE

    A VALENTINE FOR VINNIE

    ONE PERFECT ROSE

    FANFARE FOR TWO

    RITA RINGS A BELL

    THE STAR ISLAND *Series*

    WHITE COLLAR GIRL

Contents

THE WHISTLE STOP MYSTERY

Chapter 1

Same
Old Place?

Barry Loomis walked down the dusty road disconsolately. She was headed in the direction of Miller's General Store, with instructions to buy a quart of milk, a box of cereal, and a loaf of bread, but there was no hurry. It was only quarter of three, and she wasn't expected home until five o'clock. The sun was warm on her back, pleasantly warm, and it shimmered on the dusty leaves and the pointed blades of grass. The whole world, as Barry looked around her, appeared to be dry and dusty. And, she thought with a sigh, dull. Dull, at least, for a twelve-year-old girl who would love a little excitement in her life.

"What a sigh!" she heard from behind her, and Barry turned quickly. It was Chris, the new boy, who was standing by the gate to the Bassett house. Chris was taller than Barry and very thin, but after two months of farm work at the Bassetts, he had at last lost his peaked look. His pale skin had turned a golden tan, and his blond hair had bleached almost white. "It *was* a sigh, wasn't it?" he asked, with a half-smile.

Barry was embarrassed. "Yes, I guess so," she said.

"What's the trouble?"

"Oh, nothing." She moved ahead slowly, wanting to end the conversation and not knowing exactly how to go about it.

"Don't you like nice warm days like this?" He stooped and picked up a handful of pebbles that he began to throw—not very skillfully, she thought—at a fence post.

"I don't mind," Barry said indifferently. "Well, I've got to go to the store for my mother."

She trudged off down the road, conscious of his blue eyes fixed on her back. For just an instant she saw herself as he must see her, short, sturdy, dressed in a faded khaki shirt and shorts, her bare brown legs covered with scratches and bites.

She was all brown, she reflected: brown hair, brown eyes, deeply tanned skin that was almost as dark as her hair already, although summer had just begun. "Brown as a Barry!" her father had said once fondly, and everyone had laughed. Everyone but Barry. She didn't think it so funny; it was dull being all brown like that especially when her pretty cousin Alicia was around, making Barry appear browner and drabber and duller than ever. Alicia would be here in Northville for her annual visit in less than three months, and already Barry was dreading the day.

Barry put Alicia's visit out of her mind, refusing to worry about it until she had to. Her thoughts drifted back to Chris. Chris was just a boy, but he was also something of a mystery in Northville. He had appeared early in April, living at the Bassetts' and going to the Northville school where he was in the sixth grade, as was Barry, although he was a little older than she was. It had been a surprise to everyone that the Bassetts should take a boy to live with them in the first place.

"Tim Bassett's cut down his farm to almost nothing, but I guess he can't take care of it by himself any longer," Mr. Loomis said thoughtfully when Barry told him about Chris. "And a strong, willing boy should be a big help to him." Barry didn't know about the new boy's willingness, but he certainly didn't look very strong, being so pale and thin and all.

"Will he stay there always?" she asked. Not that she cared. If there was going to be someone her own age next door, why couldn't it be a girl? Barry didn't like boys on general principles. As it was, the only person her own age who lived nearby was also a boy—Lester Graham, pale and pudgy, who was forever trying to make friends with her, even though she consistently, and often very rudely, rebuffed him. Chris at least was an improvement on Lester.

"Mary and Tim are pretty old to bring up a youngster," Mrs. Loomis remarked. "I feel sorry for the boy—he won't have much fun living with two old people who aren't used to children and who are pretty much set in their ways."

Just knowing nothing about Chris Clark's background made him interesting, that and the fact that he had lived somewhere else. Barry herself had never lived anywhere but in the white-painted frame house sprawling along the top of a low hill and entirely surrounded by trees and bushes. From the road, the house could hardly be seen. Visitors turned in by the white mailbox that said "Loomis" in fat green letters, and drove between tangled thickets that made newcomers think there couldn't possibly be a house in such a wilderness. The very first bend, however, revealed the white house tucked securely amid carefully pruned trees and artfully arranged shrubs. It was a pleasant house, both inside and out, and Barry loved it.

She liked Northville too, except for moments like this one or when her cousin Alicia was there to make fun of it, calling it a whistle stop.

"What's a whistle stop?" Barry asked her father crossly, after Alicia had used the annoying term the second time. She was sure it wasn't complimentary.

"It's a place so small the trains stop only on signal," her father replied. "Why?"

"Oh, nothing." Then she added angrily, "That's what Alicia calls Northville."

"So what?" He shrugged.

Barry tried to pretend it didn't matter, but it did. Now, walking along slowly, she looked around at the town, seeing it as she so often did with Alicia's eyes. She had already crossed the bridge over North River, and was now passing the big barn of a building that was occupied entirely by the Loomis Hay, Grain, and Feed Company, owned by her father, who sold farm machinery as well as feed. Fleetingly she thought of stopping in to see him, but there was a truck outside, and an old car was just pulling up, so she knew he must be busy. She went on by the drugstore that carried almost everything Miller's General Store didn't; Milly's Lunch, with four square tables and six stools lined up at a counter; Mr. Taylor's filling station; and finally reached the shabby square building that was her destination.

Mr. Miller himself was working in the grocery end of the store this afternoon. Barry liked Mr. Miller, and she smiled at him now and said clearly, because he didn't hear very well, "A loaf of white bread, a box of cornflakes—a large one, please—and a quart of milk."

Mr. Miller stared down at Barry, nodded solemnly, and went behind the counter. Barry looked around with interest. She waved at Mrs. Taylor, who was talking excitedly to Mrs. Bassett, and noticed that everyone in the store was chattering away with unusual animation. What, she wondered, could anyone find to get so excited about in Northville?—and was immediately ashamed. You sound like Alicia, she scolded herself silently. They're just gossiping. As usual.

"Here you are," said Mr. Miller, and Barry turned back to the counter. The three objects he had placed there for her looked odd, although at first she couldn't say why. She looked more closely. "But Mr. Miller, I said cornflakes," Barry reminded him. It wasn't like Mr. Miller to make mistakes. "These are rice flakes."

"Oh," said Mr. Miller. He picked up the big box and turned back to the shelves behind him.

"And this isn't the kind of milk we usually get. The top is green; ours is orange," Barry protested.

"Oh," said Mr. Miller again. He put the milk bottle back in the big refrigerated case, and Barry thought, oh, maybe it's just the kind we get delivered that has the orange top. But no, I'm sure— She was relieved to see Mr. Miller put an orange-capped bottle in place of the other.

"And I—I wanted white bread," Barry almost wailed, seeing "Light Rye" clearly printed on the wrapper of the loaf on the counter.

"Oh," said Mr. Miller a third time, and made the exchange.

Barry was puzzled. Not only did Mr. Miller seldom make mistakes, but he usually talked a great deal. In fact, one of the problems of dealing with Mr. Miller was that it was so difficult to get away from him.

Barry bobbed her head at Mrs. Miller as she passed the dry goods counter, but Mrs. Miller, usually so friendly and cheerful, didn't even see her. She was leaning on the counter talking earnestly to two women who were bent toward her, listening intently. Just outside the door, Barry saw half a dozen men whom she knew, also deep in some sort of discussion. She edged by and heard, "Yeah, but some fella from Bedford was out here and he said——" "That's right, maybe four, five thousand an acre——" "Hear they been buying it up for months, secret-like——"

Barry shrugged. Whatever it was, by tomorrow they'd all have forgotten it, she thought. She walked down the road, shifting the awkward bag back and forth, having difficulty seeing over it.

"Going my way, lady?" she heard.

"Daddy!" Barry scrambled into the car beside her father. "How come you're going home so early?"

"Just got tired of it all," he teased her. "What's the matter— did we run out of supplies again?"

"Just bread and milk," Barry said. "And cereal. What's everybody yak-yakking about?" she asked. "Seems to me everyone in town was in the store, and all of them talking a mile a minute."

"Tell you when we get home," he said, and Barry looked at him curiously. Whatever it was, it had her father excited too, and that meant there was something to get excited about!

Mr. Loomis seemed to have no desire to talk on the short ride home. He drove into the yard, took the grocery bag from Barry's arms, and led the way to the kitchen.

"George!" exclaimed Barry's mother. "What a pleasant surprise. You're not sick?" she asked anxiously.

"Never felt better in my life," he told her cheerfully. "Good heavens, Ann, a man can close up his own business an hour early once in a while, can't he?"

"I've been telling you for years that he can," Mrs. Loomis answered with spirit. "But usually you don't hear a word I say! What is it, George?"

"Big news." He washed his hands at the sink, dried them carefully, and turned toward his wife and daughter. "And I *think* it's on the level this time, although you can't be too sure. We've had rumors before," he added, grinning.

"What's on the level?" demanded Mrs. Loomis.

"Well, you know they've been fooling around with Route 118 for years now," he said slowly. "First they were going to run it north of Bedford, then south, and then right through the middle of the city—now that was a hot one! Well, it seems to be pretty much settled. John Carroll has a cousin in the state house, and he called him, and the cousin said yes, it was really true this time!"

"What was really true?"

"They're going to bring the road right through Northville," Mr. Loomis said dramatically. Barry gulped with disappointment. She couldn't see much to get excited about in *that* piece of news.

"Through Northville!" Mrs. Loomis exclaimed. "But what's the point? I thought they were going to avoid towns; make it one of those speed highways or something. Why would they send it right through Northville?"

"Northville won't slow it up too much." Mr. Loomis chuckled. "There's a good reason, though. You know that north-south turnpike they voted an appropriation for last year? It was supposed to run about fifteen miles west of here. Well, they're going to move that one east a way, for one reason or another, and as a result, 118 and 17, or whatever they'll call it, will cross here. Right here in Northville!"

"Cross here? Why, George, that'll make Northville——"

"This will be an important crossroad." He nodded, looking pleased and at the same time solemn. "So, Barry, you can tell Alicia to put that in her pipe and smoke it. What is it she calls Northville—a whistle stop? Wait till she sees it a year from now. She won't know the place. This summer, even!"

For the first time Barry found the news interesting. Every year during Alicia's three-week visit to Northville, Barry suffered from Alicia's acid comments. Bedford, where Alicia lived, was a city. Bedford had everything—movies, big shops, huge supermarkets, beauty salons, ten-cent stores, fine restaurants. And Northville, the whistle stop, had none of these things. Barry visited Alicia and her family each winter so she knew Bedford, and she didn't think it was so wonderful, but Alicia, when Barry tried to point out this flaw or that, always had an answer to everything. On the other hand, Barry had never been able to defend Northville properly.

Now her brown eyes sparkled as she thought of Alicia's amazement when she saw Northville suddenly turned into a city even bigger and more grand than Bedford.

"Will we have a stadium?" she asked. "And a municipal auditorium? And an airport?"

"Heavens no. None of those things. Northville will never become a city, if that's what you mean. But there will be a lot going on here pretty soon. There'll be restaurants and motels—one of each, at least, and probably more—and filling stations. All sorts of things. And lots and lots of new people will move to town, and business will be better for all of us, and——"

Barry stared at her father in dismay and stopped listening. Who needed a new filling station? she grumbled to herself. Alicia wasn't going to get excited about *that*. She bit her lip in vexation. Finally she heard her father say, "——good for my business almost immediately, because real estate will go up first of all. There'll be the land-taking, to begin with, and they'll be subdividing some of the big properties and selling off parcels. Northville will really boom, Ann—at last."

Barry glanced at Mrs. Loomis, and to her surprise saw a worried look on her mother's face.

"George," she said, and there was a note in her voice that matched the expression in her eyes, "George, I hope this boom won't—well, you know—stir up the old trouble. It's been buried for so long. Do you think it will?"

Chapter 2

The First Sign

It took several days for Barry to put the bits and pieces together, and to get some idea of what was really going to happen to the town, but the "old trouble," which of course was the most exciting part of it all, remained a mystery.

Her parents answered her pointed questions with, "Oh, that's ancient history, Barry. Happened before our time even." Or, "By now everyone in town has forgotten what it was all about. You'd better forget it too." But you haven't forgotten, Barry raged silently, knowing full well that she wasn't going to get anything out of them, no matter how hard she tried.

Secretly, Barry was sure that the mystery had something to do with the Parrish place, since it was such a gloomy old mansion. No one had lived in it for years and it was strictly off limits for Barry and her friends. There was a fence around the estate, and Barry knew it was possible to get over or under or through it in spots, because some of the boys at school—even Lester Graham, although she didn't believe *him*—had boasted that they had suc-

ceeded. But she herself had never tried. The forbidden and unknown had great appeal for her, and it was quite natural for her
immediately to connect this new mystery with the Parrish place,
which was an old mystery in her own mind. Some day, she
thought, she would again ask Chris about the Parrish house.

Once, a few weeks ago, she had mentioned it to him, and had
been surprised at the anger on his face when he turned and said,
"Why would I go to that dumb old place? It's all shut up, isn't
it?"

"Well, yes." So he knew that much! "But lots of kids get in
there. Boys, I mean. I'm not allowed."

"Why do you want to know if I've been?"

"Just—just curious."

"And what if I had?"

"I thought maybe you'd tell me about it," Barry replied humbly. "What it looks like up close. If it's—spooky."

"Spooky?"

"It looks spooky from the road. So dark and—and dead-look-
ing. Maybe it's haunted." She shot a glance at his stony face. "I
just wondered," she added lamely.

Looking back, Barry decided Chris had been angry because he
hadn't been there and hated to admit it. By this time, surely he
would have climbed the forbidden fence and he'd *want* to talk
about it, just to show off. She'd ask him the very next time they
met.

One day in Miller's, she caught a glimpse of him just leaving
the store, and she waited impatiently for Mrs. Miller to fill the
Loomis order in her fussy, exasperating way. Finally, clutching
the unwieldy bag, she ran down the road after Chris. She was
lucky. He had stopped on the stone bridge and was gazing
thoughtfully into the shallow brown water of North River below.

"Hi!" panted Barry, trying not to sound as though she'd been
running, and failing miserably.

"Hello." Chris turned and looked at her with a half-smile. "What's the rush?"

"Oh, nothing." Barry shifted the bag to her other arm, then put it down on the top of the stone railing.

"Here, I'll swap you." Chris handed over a small bag and took hers. "I thought farm families bought supplies once a year or something," he teased. "I see you going to the store every couple of days. I bought an oil can," he added hastily. "Ours rusted out."

"We're not a farm family," Barry said stiffly. "Mother and Daddy used to live in Bedford. Daddy did anyway. Mother lived in Colebrook until she went to Bedford to teach school. That's where they met." Her breath was coming back, and she felt annoyed with Chris for challenging her in this way.

Chris stared moodily down into the rippling water. "I lived in Colebrook once," he said.

Barry looked at him quickly. Maybe she was going to learn something about this strange boy at last. "For long?" she asked tentatively.

"No."

"When you were little?"

"Sort of."

I'm not getting anywhere, she thought in despair. "Well, come on, we'd better go," she said, swinging the little bag carelessly, feeling the curved spike of the oil can through the paper. "Are you excited about the new roads?"

Chris threw her a piercing glance. "Excited! You mean pleased? I think it's awful," he said shortly.

"Awful? But why?"

"Wait till you see what they do to this town," Chris announced. "You just wait. And they'll mess everything up—for all of us."

"What do you mean?"

"You'll see." He obviously intended to say nothing more, and they walked on in silence. When they reached the Bassetts' old stone gate, he solemnly exchanged packages with Barry and turned through the crumbling pillars without a word. What's with him? Barry asked herself. He just doesn't like to *talk* about new roads even. I wonder why?

At home, she looked inside the box and found that the mail had come. There was a letter for her from Alicia. Alicia's letters usually had the same effect on Barry that Alicia herself did, but this time she opened the envelope almost eagerly, expecting that at last her cousin had been put in her place by Barry's announcement of the new roads.

"Daddy says now Northville will be a whistle stop on a big road instead of a whistle stop on a little one," Alicia wrote in her prim handwriting. "What's so great about that?"

Alicia's father and Barry's father were brothers, and they were always teasing each other. Barry's mother had once told her it was just their way and that they enjoyed it, but Barry didn't think it was all very funny. Hurt, she read that part of Alicia's letter to her father that evening, but he just grinned and said, "Write the belle of Bedford to tell her pop he's going to wish he'd come here after all." The message didn't make any sense to Barry, so she decided to forget it. She felt she should be on firmer ground whenever she matched wits with Alicia.

It was amazing to Barry to see how quickly the town began to change. Bulldozers and other pieces of heavy machinery were already at work, turning land that had been covered with grass and weeds and dusty trees into squares of raw yellow dirt. Huge trucks drove up and dumped great piles of brick, lumber, and cement blocks everywhere. By asking questions and keeping her ears open, Barry learned that in this spot there would be a filling station, in that a motel, over here a restaurant, and so on. But the first time she was able to fit the jigsaw pieces together was one day when she drove out into the country with her father.

"What a mess!" she wailed. "What will Alicia say?"

Her father looked at her sharply. "When are you and Alicia going to grow up and be friends?"

"But we are friends. We're best friends," Barry protested.

"Um." He glanced at her as he swung the car over to the right, following a crooked arrow drawn on a detour sign. "Everywhere you go, construction," he grumbled, yanking the wheel this way and that in an effort to miss the worst ruts. Barry looked around with interest. They were driving along a dusty track that led them right through a field behind the Goulds' house. From the back, the buildings of the town, without the familiar signs and displays of merchandise that she saw on Main Street, were dismal indeed. For a moment she could see why Alicia was so scornful of Northville.

"How come we never saw the town from here before?" she asked sadly.

"Because we never drove through the Goulds' back pasture before, and I hope we never do again. This car couldn't take it twice." Her father grunted as a front wheel hit an especially deep hole. "Now, see over there, where that big tank is? That'll be a filling station. The Goulds sold the land just the other day. Didn't take them long to start working on it, did it? Barry, this is all very good for Northville. For me, even. Property is in demand, all of a sudden. Apart from the taking of certain strips of it for the highways, all sorts of people from outside want lots, to build filling stations and motels and the rest. The Goulds have been trying for years to scrape enough cash together to buy a new tractor so they could turn over more land and farm it. They sold that little piece there for the filling station and it more than paid for the tractor. Now I'll sell them more seed and fertilizer. See how it works?"

"Oh, Daddy, will we be rich? Could we buy the Parrish house?"

"Sorry, Barry, not a chance. Rich? That was just one example —it won't be as easy as all that. And why that old house? We couldn't afford a mansion like that even if we wanted it, which we certainly don't."

Barry bit her lip. She had hoped to trick her father into telling her something about the Parrish place. For once, he paid no attention to her attempt to get something out of him and went on, "Look at the skeleton of the motel from here. Pretty big, I'd say. That was where that old——" he stopped, carefully adjusted the sunshield over his head and finished "——that old frame house was. They pulled it down when you were little."

Barry stared at her father. The old wooden house had been a mystery too, now that she thought of it. No one had lived there in her lifetime, and the house itself, a little off Main Street, had been something to hurry by unless it was broad daylight. Wooden shutters were closed over the windows and there were always bits of paper drifting or whirling around the neglected yard. The old tumble-down house and the big Parrish house were connected, vaguely, in her mind.

"Who does the land belong to?" she asked, wondering for the first time who could own a stretch of land that had been nothing but dust and weeds for so long.

"Some relative of—the previous owner," Mr. Loomis told her. "Cousin, maybe. I forget. Never paid any attention to the place all these years, but I'll bet he was glad enough to sell it and get a good price for it."

"Will the motel be finished while Alicia is here?"

"Not if she goes home on Labor Day, as usual," her father said grinning. "But they build things so fast these days, it'll look like a motel, at least. Maybe she'll stay longer though. Would you like that?"

Barry shrugged. He knew very well that three weeks of Alicia was all she could take, she thought resentfully. And the same could be said of Alicia's attitude toward Northville. Still, this year would be different!

Even her own home was going to be a little different, she discovered that afternoon. Mrs. Loomis greeted them with the announcement that she was going to Bedford the next day to buy material for new draperies for all the downstairs rooms.

"Oh, Ann, what's the rush?" Mr. Loomis demanded. "Just because business is good all of a sudden."

"I've been wanting them for years," Barry's mother said calmly. "And now I'm going to have them."

"But what's the hurry?" Her husband looked at her sharply. "Oh, I get it. You know, you're as bad as Barry. Just because Ed and Diana will be here for a weekend in August?"

"Everything will be finished just in time," Mrs. Loomis said serenely. "Mrs. Atkins will be in day after tomorrow to help me make them. I think we'd better do some painting too—Barry's old nursery especially. And, Barry, I know your own room could stand a little fixing up."

"Before Alicia comes?"

"Before Alicia comes," her mother promised her. "Oh, I telephoned Mary Bassett just now and invited Chris Clark to go along with us next Thursday. He doesn't have much fun."

Barry bristled. Chris was all right, but she was sure she didn't want him along on the Fourth of July picnic. Still, there was nothing she could do about it.

The Fourth was a lovely day, sunny and warm, and Barry was surprised to find out what good company Chris was. He was at ease with all of them and seemed to enjoy everything. On the way home, he began to tell Barry about watching the men working on the new roads.

"I thought you weren't excited about the roads," she said accusingly.

"I'm not. I like to watch all that big machinery, but I hate to think what those roads will do to this nice little town," Chris said.

"I'm afraid Chris is right about that." Barry jumped as her father spoke. "Making a small town over in this way is bound to attract a whole lot of new people, and some of them won't be the kind you'd go out and shop for, if you were looking for nice neighbors."

Chris nodded, his face solemn in the pale light. Barry thought he looked relieved, as though he had been afraid Mr. Loomis was going to say something else.

"Not only the new ones, but I can think of a few 'old' people I'd just as soon not see back here," Mrs. Loomis said. She was talking to Barry's father, and seemed to have forgotten the two riding in the back of the car. "From what I've heard——" She caught a warning gesture from her husband then, glanced back at Barry, and quickly launched into a dull little tale about a cleaning woman who had, two years before, disappeared with six of the Loomis spoons.

She didn't mean Mrs. Brennan when she started, Barry thought wisely. She meant someone else. Or maybe several people. And it's got something to do with that mysterious "old trouble" again. I'm sure of it.

Chapter   3

Alicia Arrives

Barry woke up on *the* morning in August thinking, Today's the day. Alicia will be here this afternoon! She made her bed with great care and picked up her room methodically. Blooming with blue rosebuds, the room looked fresh and pretty, pretty enough even for Alicia, whose bedroom in Bedford was pink and ruffled, but much smaller than this one.

The whole house looked nice, Barry decided, wandering around to take one last look before lunch. Even her mother was pleased with it, and her father had stopped complaining about "all this foolishness" so she knew he must like it too. The old nursery had been painted and papered, but there was no furniture in it. Barry closed the door on the empty room and idly wondered why her parents had bothered to have it done at all. They didn't need another bedroom. Alicia shared Barry's, when she was here, and Uncle Ed and Aunt Diana would use the spacious guest room for the few nights they would be in Northville.

It was nearly four o'clock when the big black car rolled into the Loomis driveway. Alicia was dressed in a pale yellow dress with a matching cardigan. Her golden-brown hair gleamed in the sun. She's grown taller, Barry thought disgustedly. She's inches taller than I am.

"Rusty!" shrieked Alicia. "Get down. Barry, get him off my brand-new dress."

Barry reached for Rusty's collar. "He's just glad to see you," she explained. "Come on, boy, you go on down to the creek and have a swim."

Somehow Barry had imagined that she would plunge right into the big subject of the new highways, but as usual Alicia got there first. They were in the bedroom, hanging up Alicia's dresses and putting the rest of her things in the dresser drawers that had been emptied for her.

"That road out from Bedford!" Alicia exclaimed. "It's dreamy. Why, we made it in less than three hours, and it always took at least four. Sometimes longer. But of course when we got almost to Northville——" She made a face. "Dust! And a horrible detour. It was awful." She patted her dress as though it were still covered with dust.

"Won't be for long," Barry said shortly. "Wait till you see what they've done, Alicia."

"We saw it," Alicia said indifferently. "Isn't our new car super? Of course it's all dusty now. Let's go downstairs—I'm finished unpacking."

Barry followed Alicia numbly. So that's all it meant to Alicia—just dust. She felt completely deflated. But then, she thought morosely, it was always like this when Alicia was here.

In the last day or two, Barry had made up her mind to say nothing to Alicia about Chris. Mysterious past or not, she decided there was no point in bringing them together, because she was sure they wouldn't get along. Chris would be her own personal secret. She had reckoned without Alicia's sharp brown eyes, though. On the second day of her visit, as they walked slowly down the road by the Bassett place, Alicia asked suddenly, "Who's that?"

"Who? Where?" Barry's heart sank. She knew very well whom Alicia meant. She had caught a glimpse of Chris's blue-and-white clothed figure at the other end of the field.

Alicia pointed. "That boy. There."

"Oh, that's just Chris." Barry shrugged.

"Chris who? Is he related to the Bassetts?"

"He lives there. Want to try to get Daddy to take us to the lake this afternoon?"

"He won't. Mother and Daddy are still here. Chris who? Bassett?"

"His name is Clark," Barry told her curtly.

"Let's go see him," Alicia suggested promptly. "I should say hello to Mrs. Bassett anyway."

Alicia turned back toward the Bassetts' gate, and there was nothing to do but follow her. As they walked, Alicia succeeded in worming out of Barry what little information she had about Chris.

"Oh, my," Alicia said, when Barry finished. "He's probably an orphan or something. And he's lived in a whole lot of places. I wonder," she added nastily, "how he likes living in this whistle stop, after all those big towns. At least I suppose they were bigger than this. Most everything is."

Barry scowled. She wondered if she'd ever hear the end of "whistle stop." "He likes it here," she said defensively. "He thinks the new roads are going to spoil Northville. He likes it the way it is."

"It won't be much different. Does he go over to your house much?"

"He doesn't have much time off," Barry told her. They had reached the Bassett house and Chris, she saw, had come from the opposite direction and was sitting in the shade by the woodpile, with his back to them. Just then Mrs. Bassett, a thin gray-haired woman, walked out of the back door.

"Hello, Mrs. Bassett," Alicia said sweetly. "I've just come to Northville for my summer visit. How are you?"

Barry was disgusted. Alicia sounded about as real, she thought angrily, as—as—well, one of Lester Graham's silly bird calls.

Mrs. Bassett appeared pleased. "I'm fine," she said. "Time for your summer visit already? Wish I had some lemonade. Like a glass of milk?"

"No, thank you," Alicia replied, still sweetly. "We're just walking around. I lose track, between visits."

Lose track of what? What's she talking about? Barry wondered.

"Well, it's nice to see you again," remarked Alicia conversationally. "Good-by now."

Barry scowled. Of all the silly expressions she had ever heard, she thought "Good-by now" was the worst.

"Come on," Alicia whispered fiercely. "She's gone inside."

Barry, who had almost forgotten the object of the visit, allowed herself to be tugged along. As they drew nearer to Chris, she began to hold back, but Alicia was firm.

"Introduce us," she whispered sternly.

Barry, embarrassed, muttered their names and ducked her head first at one and then the other. Alicia looked at Chris with interest; he returned her gaze calmly. Just as Barry was about to say, "Oh, come on, Alicia, let's go home," Chris surprised her by saying, "Sit down, why don't you? It's cool right here. I have to go back to work in a minute." He smiled right at Barry, and she felt better.

"Feel that breeze," remarked Alicia, sitting down on the grass as gracefully as though she had on some kind of fluffy dance

dress and ballet slippers instead of navy linen shorts and sneak-ers. "They tell me you used to live in Colebrook."

Chris shrugged and said, "Yes, I did for a while."

"Where else have you lived?" Alicia inquired. "I mean——"

"Lots of places. Most of them awful. Well," he added, stand-ing up quickly, "I've got to go back and finish the job."

His blue eyes flicked across Alicia's face and rested a moment on Barry's. He smiled and, in a moment, was gone.

"Rude." Alicia sniffed. Then she giggled. "Well, at least he's better than that awful Lester Graham!"

The next day, Barry's mother took the girls up to Lake Tri-mount. As soon as they got there, Mrs. Loomis went down the beach to talk to some friends, and the cousins, after a time in the water, stretched out on the sand together.

"Barry," Alicia said slowly, "do you suppose Chris has got any-thing to do with—you know."

Barry, who had been staring at the sand just under her nose, sat up quickly. "With what?" she demanded.

"With the mystery. With whatever it is that nobody will talk about in this town," Alicia said calmly.

Barry clenched her fists in dismay. Ever since Alicia's arrival she had been forcing herself to keep quiet about the "old trou-ble," because she felt sure Alicia would sneer at it, reduce it to nothing. At the same time she had wanted to share the secret, thinking what fun it would be if the two of them could ferret out the mystery—maybe even solve it.

But she had kept quiet, and here was Alicia coming right out with it. There was no doubt in Barry's mind but that Alicia's words referred to the "old trouble."

Before Barry could think of anything to say, Alicia turned to her and said, "Gee, I'm sorry. Daddy said I was never to mention it to you, because he wasn't sure how much you knew about it."

"I don't know anything about it," Barry said crossly. "And I don't see how you do. You don't even live in Northville."

"Probably that's *why* I know," Alicia suggested. "Nobody told me either. I just happened to hear Daddy telling a friend of his about it. When he found out I was in the next room and had heard what he said, he was absolutely furious, and he made me promise not to mention it to you. And I never did until this minute, did I?"

"I'll never let on, I promise," Barry said. "Gee, Alicia, I'm glad you know. Please tell me what you heard. I've been just bursting to say something to you about it, but I really don't know what it's all about. Tell," she begged.

"I don't really know much." Barry, watching her cousin's pretty face, thought that for once Alicia wasn't conscious of herself at all. She was so interested in what she was going to say that she frowned and bit her lip in a most unbecoming way. And for the first time, Barry found herself really fond of Alicia—probably the very first time ever!

"It's something about that funny old house," Alicia said carefully. "What was the name of the people who lived there? Paris?"

"Parrish. I knew it!" Barry clapped her hands together softly. "Oh, do go on."

"Well, that family lived there for a long time. And then the son of the man who lived in the house last got killed there somehow—that part I don't know about at all. Daddy didn't say. He just told his friend 'and after young Philip Parrish's death, the family moved away for good.' Something like that."

"But what else did he say?"

"Only that Northville's 'trouble,' I think that's what he called it, was that it was a border town, and had a lot of bad people running around. I remember he said, 'I wouldn't want to risk running into trouble with my help right from the beginning,' and then he said something about Bedford and——"

"Oh!" cried Barry. "I guess I know what that part means. I think your father once planned to live here himself."

"Here? How ever do you know that?"

"Never mind now," Barry said impatiently. "It's not important."

"Well, it does fit. I kind of remember they were talking about how come Daddy had decided to build his factory in East Bedford."

"But go on," Barry urged her, "about the mystery. What is it?"

"That's just the trouble," Alicia said. "I don't know. But there was one—and that must be why Daddy didn't want to build his factory here. And it had something to do with Northville being close to the Canadian border and with the Parrish place and some people who used to live here. Isn't it exciting?"

"I guess so," Barry said doubtfully. "But—well, if we don't even know what it is——"

"We'll find out!" Alicia exclaimed. "And while I'm here! We'll be like detectives in the movies and we'll find out. And maybe Chris will help."

"Chris?" Barry asked blankly.

"Why, of course. He's mixed up in it; I just know it. You wait and see. So of course he'll help us. And we'll help him."

Chapter 4

The Parrish Place

"But how can we figure out anything about it if we don't even see it?" complained Alicia. The cousins had just walked along Main Street and had turned down the dirt road that led to the house itself. They took elaborate pains not to show that they were trying to see more than the odd little turret on top of the weatherbeaten old mansion.

"I don't know. But we can't go in there and you know it."

Alicia kicked angrily at a stone. Barry had explained that long ago her parents had stated, "You are *never* to go over or under or through the fence around that old house. We know that children do get in, from time to time, but they are *not* supposed to. It's private property to begin with, and as far as you're concerned it's definitely off limits. Do you understand?"

"They never told me not to go in," Alicia muttered. "I'll go by myself some day."

"You'd better not," Barry warned her.

"That fence doesn't look so old," Alicia said fretfully. "Ugly metal thing. How long ago did this family disappear anyway?"

Barry shrugged. "About the time I was born, I guess, or a little before."

"Let's ask Chris to go for us."

"You can go ahead and ask Chris if you want to. I spoke to him about it twice, and he nearly bit my head off."

"Do you think he's afraid to go in?"

"No, of course not," Barry scoffed. "But he might be scared that the Bassetts would find out about it. I think they're kind of strict."

Alicia sighed. They turned, reluctantly, back toward Main Street. The road to the Parrish house turned off about half a mile west of the spot where the big intersection of the two highways was to be, and it ran all the way down to North River, but since part of the Parrish property had been fenced off, the road appeared to end at the locked gate in the tall metal fence. Barry's father had told her that the land that belonged to the big gloomy house actually extended all the way out to the main road, but that only the thickly wooded part, where the house and other buildings were, had been closed in behind the fence. The only thing that could be seen now were the remains of a small brick-yard, half on one side of the fence and half on the other.

Barry and Alicia crossed Main Street and walked along the other side, staring with great interest at the motel being built on the southwest corner of the intersection. The shell of the building was there, looking square and substantial, but the windows were still empty, and the ground all around raw and dusty.

"And there," said Alicia, pointing to a spot just behind the new motel, "is where a funny old character lived in a funny old house. Let's go poke around," she suggested hopefully.

"They won't let us near the motel," Barry reminded her. "Afraid we'll fall into a hole or something. And besides, I spent hours there, before they started building it. There wasn't anything to see at all. The house hadn't even had a cellar."

Alicia sighed again. "Hi, Chris!" she called suddenly, scrambling over a fence and trotting across the meadow to where Chris Clark was moving along slowly. Chris stopped and looked back, smiling. He waited patiently as the girls hurried up. "Where's the fire?" he asked pleasantly. "It's too hot to rush around. Why aren't you two swimming or something?"

"That's what I'd like to know," Barry grumbled.

"Chris, we want your help." Alicia sat down on the broken stone wall, carefully selecting the only place that was shaded by a gnarled old apple tree. "Sit down a minute. Look, have you ever been on the Parrish place?"

Chris glanced quickly at the Bassett house, although they were well out of earshot. Then he nodded with pride.

"Twice," he said.

"Tell us about it," Alicia begged. "Is it awful?"

"No. No, it's real nice," he said slowly. "Oh, it's a mess; I mean around the house, all bushes and trees and tall grass. It hasn't been taken care of in years, but it must have been great once. The house sits up on a little hill, with the river down below and everything."

"But did you get *into* the house?" Alicia demanded.

"Of course not. That would be breaking and entering, wouldn't it?"

"Well, climbing over the fence is trespassing," Alicia retorted. "Isn't it?"

He grinned sheepishly. "I guess so."

"Some of the kids at school have been inside the house," Barry said.

"Are you sure?" Chris looked angry.

"They said so," Barry assured him airily.

"Why don't you, Chris?" Alicia prodded.

Chris stood up and began restlessly piling fallen stones on top of one another, as though he intended to repair the old wall. "What would I look for if I did go in?"

"We don't know," Barry said. "But there's some mystery—— Well, we thought if we could just look around, we might find out something. But I don't know what we'd be looking for."

For a moment she thought Chris was going to laugh at her, but he just smiled and said, "OK, I get it. As soon as I can, I'll go 'look around' and I'll report back to you. But don't get mad at me if I don't find anything."

"How soon can you go?" Alicia asked. "I'm only going to be here until Labor Day, you know." For once she's going to be sorry to leave, Barry thought with amazement. It didn't seem possible!

"I'll go tomorrow. The Bassetts will be in Colebrook all day, and I'm caught up with my work. Or I will be if I get going again." He stood up, and without another word loped off down the field beyond the stone wall. Alicia and Barry turned in the opposite direction and followed the faint path by the creek toward the Loomis house.

"Now we can go swimming," Barry said thankfully. "I'm *hot*."

"We-ell," Alicia agreed grudgingly. "For just a little while. But I'm going to find out something about that old torn-down house, somehow. Then when Chris tells us what he's found, we can fit it together."

"Oh, Alicia, you don't make any sense," Barry objected. "He may not find out a thing. And we're not sure the two houses are connected anyway."

"I bet they are," Alicia told her stubbornly.

"And who's going to tell you anything about an old house that was pulled down years ago?"

"Mrs. Miller. She likes me. And she talks a lot," Alicia said sweetly.

Barry agreed that Mrs. Miller was the greatest talker in the whole town, and it was true that Alicia seemed to have wound the elderly woman around her little finger.

But suddenly Barry was bored with the whole thing. "You go ahead," she said crossly. "I'm going to spend the whole afternoon at the creek, getting cool."

"All right." Alicia's cheeks were pink. "You do that. And I guess I'll go down to the store right now."

They parted in anger, Barry heading back for the house and her swimsuit, and Alicia turning toward the dusty road. Barry looked back at her and saw that her cousin walked stiffly, her head high. I hope she gets sunstroke, Barry said savagely to herself, but she soon found that paddling in the shallow creek, with only Rusty for company, wasn't much fun any more. She had, in just a few days, become accustomed to having Alicia always there, chattering and giggling, and in spite of herself, she found her mind turning constantly to Miller's store and whatever Alicia might be finding out.

It was an incredibly long afternoon. Nothing but the stubborn streak Barry's father said she was born with kept her at the creek for two whole hours. Even Rusty wanted to go back to the house long before Barry decided it was time to leave the shallow stream, which was called, on the map, Minnow Brook. Alicia, she found, had been home only a few minutes when Barry, hot again from having unconsciously hurried all the way, ran into the kitchen.

"Hi," said Alicia, her shining eyes flicking warningly to Mrs. Loomis' back. "You were right, it was too hot down there. Thanks for the lemonade, Aunt Ann. Come on, Barry. First for the shower—I'm hotter than you are."

Barry silently took the glass of lemonade her mother held out to her and followed Alicia upstairs, expecting to hear the shower running. Instead, her cousin was standing in the middle of their bedroom, twisting her hands in excitement.

"Oh, Barry, you should have been there. Close the door, huh? Mrs. Miller really talks a mile a minute, doesn't she?" She giggled as she began to unbutton her blouse. "I do need that shower," she confessed. "I practically ran all the way home."

"But what did you find out?" Barry peeled off her damp swimsuit and tossed it in the corner with a complete disregard of the house rules. Then she sat down, wrapped in her terry robe. "Tell, Alicia."

"Well, you remember I heard Daddy say that this Philip Parrish had died somehow, and that was why the family moved away? Or I guess it was why. Anyway, they moved just at that time. Well, the man who lived in that funny little house left town at the very same moment!"

"Did Mrs. Miller tell you that?"

"She told me more than that!" Alicia exclaimed dramatically. "She said Uncle Louis—that was what the man who lived there was called—left Northville in July, 1957. So I said, 'Why, Mrs. Miller, what a wonderful memory you have! Imagine remembering a date like that all this time!' She just kind of blushed and said, 'Well, anybody in town would know that date, Alice.' She always calls me Alice," Alicia complained.

"Never mind that. Go *on*!"

"So of course I said, 'Why, Mrs. Miller?' And she kind of fussed around a minute and then she said, 'Because that was when it happened—poor young Phil Parrish and all.' And then Mr. Miller came up and glared at her and at me, and I just kind of ran out. I forgot the crayons I asked her for, too."

Barry stared at Alicia and said, "But it doesn't seem to—to prove much of anything. Just that one man happened to leave town at the same time another one died. That old man used to work in the Parrish brickyard, I think. Maybe there wasn't any more work."

"I never saw anybody making any old bricks," Alicia objected.

"Daddy said it was a very busy place once," Barry reported. "Years ago. Every chimney in town was made out of those bricks, and all those brick houses out East Northville way. But it seems that when Philip Parrish's father died, they kind of let it go, except for one man who worked there and who still puttered around some. Then probably after Philip Parrish died, this man —Uncle Louis—didn't have any more work, so he just left."

"Or maybe he *had* to leave," Alicia cried. "Maybe he—maybe he killed that Philip Parrish!"

Barry frowned over this while her cousin was in the shower, feeling sure that Alicia was reading something into the situation that wasn't there. Apparently Alicia had been doing some thinking on her own, too, because as soon as she emerged from the bathroom, briskly towelling her curly light-brown hair, she said, "Look, maybe there isn't even any connection. But there might be. Mrs. Miller thought of the two things together. Not much happens in this town year after year, but to have two things happen at the same time—there really has to be a connection, don't you think? Now all we've got to do is find out what the connection is."

Barry nodded and headed glumly for her own shower. She was disappointed. Somehow she had expected more of Alicia. When she returned to the bedroom, Alicia, looking cool and neat in a pretty pink shift, had more news for her.

"I forgot to tell you that when I went into the store, Mrs. Miller was talking to Mrs. Gould. And guess what? Mrs. Gould has rented rooms to people who wanted to stay at the motel though it isn't even ready. Isn't that a scream?"

Barry looked at her cousin with exasperation. Alicia's bits of information seemed to impress Alicia, but Barry thought this nugget even more disappointing than the other.

"New people!" Alicia pointed out. "Imagine three people wanting to come here to stay. Gee, Barry, I'm awfully glad I came this summer. You were right when you said the new roads were going to make a difference. The old whistle stop was never like this!"

Chapter 5

Strangers
in Town

They had counted on Chris for a really exciting news report, but Chris let them down. Although he had promised to visit the Parrish place the very next day after they talked to him, he later told them curtly that the Bassetts had taken him to Colebrook with them, and since then he'd been too busy.

"He acted as though it wasn't even important," Barry stormed. "The next time we ask *him* to help!"

"He's all we've got," Alicia reminded her. "Come on, let's go down to the store and see if we can find out anything about the people who are living at the Goulds'."

The cousins were luckier with this part of their endeavor. One thing seemed to lead to another, and after an hour of poking around, talking to people here and there and trying to look aimless and innocent, they found they had learned a little more. They had even met or seen the people involved.

The first stranger, one of three living at the Goulds', they spied at Taylor's filling station. Alicia had clutched Barry and muttered, "That's one of them. He just drove out of the Goulds' back yard. Ooh, isn't he *handsome!*"

Barry nodded and walked up to Mr. Taylor. "When does Judy get home?" she asked, and then didn't listen as he explained patiently, in his slow drawl, what Barry already knew—that Judy would leave the small hotel where she was waiting on tables a week after Labor Day.

"Place closes up, but they told her she could stay on a few days to earn a little more money," he said. "Guess she plans on getting a lot of new clothes, now she'll be going to college."

Alicia, who had been standing just behind Barry, suddenly edged up front. She batted her eyelashes at the stranger and murmured to Mr. Taylor, "Oh, it must be wonderful to go to college!"

The stranger, leaning on his car, smiled down at her.

"Won't be very long before you're there too, young lady," he said. "Once they start, they grow up in a hurry, don't they, Ralph?"

Alicia threw Barry a look that said, "They know each other!" Barry nodded briefly, dug two dimes out of the pocket of her shorts and without a word went to the coke machine, where she pretended to have trouble opening one of the bottles. When she returned, the stranger was just pulling away.

"Who's he, Mr. Taylor?" Alicia asked.

"Name's Kenyon. Paul Kenyon. Staying over at Sadie Gould's for a spell."

"Why?"

"Why?" Mr. Taylor looked at Alicia in astonishment. "Why? I don't know why. Wants to stay in town and the motel's not finished yet. Guess that's why."

Barry came to her cousin's rescue. "Alicia can't see why anyone would want to stay in Northville," she said with a giggle. "You have to have a reason, she means."

"Well, I don't know what his reason is. But he asks a lot of questions—just like you kids," he added with a grin.

"About what?"

"About who, mostly." Mr. Taylor stared down at Alicia with a puzzled frown. "Come to think of it, he is kind of curious about the people who live here. And especially the people moving in. Like the Marbles—people like that."

"Who are the Marbles?" Alicia and Barry asked together.

"'Own the motel. You kids are real question machines!" he finished, and then turned toward a car that had just pulled up beside the gas pump.

Barry and Alicia swallowed the rest of their cokes quickly, put the bottles in the rack, and headed, without a word, for the motel. They had been cautioned often enough not to get too close to the bulldozers and other pieces of equipment, but now the men were working on the interior, and Barry thought the rules no longer applied. There was a tall man standing in front of one of the doors, talking to two workmen in dusty overalls. Alicia without hesitation led the way, and the girls reached him just as the workmen walked away.

"Hello," said Alicia with her best smile. "I'm Alicia Loomis and this is my cousin Barry. Barry lives in Northville, and I'm visiting. Do you mind if we look at your new motel? It's beautiful."

The man, who had heavy shoulders and close-cut reddish hair, smiled at her. Everyone smiles at Alicia, Barry thought.

"Not much to see," he said cheerfully. "But look around. Just don't get in the way of the workmen. OK?"

"Oh, we wouldn't get in the way," Alicia promised. "It's so exciting having a motel here! Isn't it, Barry? How did you happen to pick Northville, Mr.—are you Mr. Marble?"

"Yep. Why not Northville? New roads and all. Besides," he added, "my wife owns this property."

"Really? Did she live here?"

"Never saw the place," the man told her. "Some old uncle of hers lived here, and when he died he left her his house. Not much of a place, though. They pulled the house down before it fell down, I guess, a while back. Michele—that's my wife—had about decided to quit paying taxes on the land when we found out about this new road-building program. So we drove out here to take a look, and what do you know? We've got ourselves some land right bang on the cloverleaf. We ran motels for a while, so we know something about it. And we're in business. Right?" He grinned at them, his face friendly and cheerful. Alicia opened her mouth to ask another question, but he wheeled suddenly and called, "OK, Ben, be right with you," and strode off toward the end of the building.

"An uncle of his wife's. That must be Uncle Louis!" Alicia exclaimed. "And he's dead. Barry, this is terrific. Where'll we go next?"

"What's so terrific?" Barry objected. "Well, we could go next door and watch them put that tank in at the new filling station. It's on the Goulds' land. I mean, the Goulds sold the land to them. Maybe we'll meet someone else staying at the Goulds'—it's right next door."

Once again the girls ran into a stranger who was talkative, although this one, they both felt, was not as friendly as the others. He was surly, rather than cheerful, and he appeared to talk more from a desire to boast than to be pleasant to them.

"My father sent me out to keep an eye on things," he said, waving his hand at the small square building. Workmen were sinking the huge black tank in the dry yellow earth in front of the station, and two gleaming red pumps were lying on their sides not far away. "Can't trust anybody, you know. My dad owns a whole bunch of these stations, and he's too busy to come himself. My name's Roy Upton. I sleep here—got a cot inside—

just for now. We may move here—rent a house or something. Kind of dull for a guy like me, though, that likes action. You kids always lived here?"

Barry for once got the answer out first, and she noticed with some gratification that the boy spoke almost exclusively to her after that. She supposed you'd call him a boy, although he could be seventeen or eighteen or even older. He was of medium height and very thin, with a sharp pointed face and bright black eyes set close together beside his thin pointed nose. She didn't like him, she knew that. There was something cold and arrogant about him, as well as something almost furtive. His faded blue shirt was torn and dirty. For some reason she found herself thinking of the clean white shirts Chris always wore, and Chris did dirty work too.

"Not much of a burg to look at," Roy said. "But it probably has quite a history. Most of these little towns do. What's the biggest thing in Northville's life anyway?"

Barry frowned at him. She had the impression that he expected a very special kind of answer. But what?

"Nothing much." She shrugged.

"Oh, I don't believe that. What about that big ark of a place over there across the road. Bet that's got a history. Secret staircases—all that guff?"

"I wouldn't know. I've never been near it," Barry retorted.

"Why is it all fenced off? Why are they trying to keep people away?"

"Because it belongs to someone who doesn't want people walking all over the lawn," Alicia snapped. "Come on, Barry, we'd better get home."

"Lawn! Are you kidding? Weeds, is more like it. And bushes going wild all over the place."

"So long," Alicia called back, grabbing Barry's hand and pulling her along. "Got to go."

Alicia waited until they'd walked back across the dirt road that ran between the filling station and the new motel. "Did you hear that? He knows all about that place! He's been there. Weeds and bushes—he must have climbed over the fence himself. Why was he asking all those questions? He probably knows the answers anyway. I didn't like him, did you? He looked mean, real mean. My father says people with eyes close together——" She broke off suddenly, and Barry followed the direction of her cousin's interested stare. A man was leaving the motel. He was a short, chunky man with a round face, and he was backing away slowly as he called to someone inside. "Well, is good to know you. Good. Louis was good friend, Michele. Glad to meet his family."

Alicia clutched Barry's arm. "Did you hear that?"

Barry nodded, and made a silent "shh" with her lips.

"No, I'm OK at the Goulds' for now. But you save me a good room, when she open. I want to be first customer, don't you forget it. Good-by, Michele."

"That's another one then," Alicia whispered. "At the Goulds'. Let's go home. I'm hungry."

Alicia acted as though they'd learned something, Barry thought resentfully, whereas from her point of view they'd found out nothing except who some of the strangers in town were.

"But don't you see," Alicia persisted, as Barry voiced her sentiments. "We have found out quite a lot. That tall handsome man, Mr. Kenyon, asks a lot of questions. You don't just move into a place and start asking questions unless you're trying to find out something special, for heaven's sake. Oh, those blue eyes—I thought I'd faint when he talked to us! And that awful boy, Roy, asked us a lot of questions, or tried to. And what's he interested in? The Parrish house! And that last man, the little fat one—he knew Uncle Louis!"

"But——"

"Just think about it. We know that the mystery is tied up with the Parrishes and Uncle Louis. So——"

Barry shrugged. "Guess I'm just the impatient type," she said finally. "Doesn't seem like much to me." Even if she couldn't see the excitement in it all that Alicia did, she was glad of one thing: Alicia was truly enjoying her visit this summer!

The next day they saw Chris.

"Hi, Chris," Alicia cried. "When are you going you-know-where?"

Chris was sitting on the Bassetts' fence, and he looked down at them in that maddeningly superior way he had sometimes.

"Tomorrow," he said. "Unless Mr. Bassett finds something else for me to do."

"Chris, be careful," Barry said. "There are a lot of other people around that probably want to go in there too. Don't let them see how you get in."

Chris scowled darkly. "Don't worry about that. What other people?" he asked as an afterthought.

Barry opened her mouth to speak, but Alicia shook her head. Barry closed her mouth, thought suddenly, I don't have to take orders from her all the time, and said quickly, "Everyone in town. All the new ones anyway."

Chris narrowed his eyes thoughtfully. "You know that man at the Goulds'—the short, fat man? I was driving along with Mr. Bassett this morning, and I saw him sneaking down the road toward the gate. Is he the one you mean?"

"Yes," Barry told him, "and the other man who lives at the Goulds'—the tall, thin one."

"With the dreamy blue eyes," Alicia put in.

Chris looked disgusted and turned back to Barry, who said, "And that Roy Upton, at the new filling station."

"Him," Chris said with scorn. "I don't like him." There was a shrill whistle from the direction of the Bassett house. "Got to go," he said, sliding off the fence. "That was Mr. Bassett. I didn't think he knew I was still here."

"Don't forget!" Alicia called after him. Chris waved a reassuring hand as he hurried away. Alicia watched him go for a minute, and then said, "Come on, let's go to the restaurant."

"Milly's? Are you hungry again?"

"Of course not, silly. I heard Mrs. Miller say Milly had a new waitress, and she's living at the Goulds'. We should see her. Can't we get cokes there?"

"I don't think Milly likes people just having cokes or coffee. But the place won't be busy at this time of day, so I guess it'll be all right." Barry put thoughts of a cooling splash in the creek out of her mind, and Alicia, watching her cousin's face, laughed.

"This won't take long," she said. "Then we'll go to the creek. OK?"

Milly had more than doubled the size of her little boxlike lunchroom. She had had a new kitchen built on the back and had used the space from the old one for the restaurant. Now, instead of four small tables, seating four people each, and a counter with six stools, the girls found ten tables sitting primly in two rows, and a long counter with a dozen stools lined up in front of it. Everything looked fresh and new, and Milly herself was busy hanging red-and-white checked curtains at the windows. Milly was a stout, good-natured woman, who turned as they walked in.

"Hi, Barry," she called. "Come to see my new place? Pretty fancy, isn't it? Look at that new counter-top. Cost me a fortune, but it ought to last longer than I do. Ellen—mind waiting on the customers? I want to finish this."

Ellen came out of the kitchen, wiping her hands on a paper towel.

"Hello," she said. "Want to sit at a table, or up at the counter?"

"At the counter," Barry said quickly. "We just want cokes. This is my cousin, Alicia." She looked at Ellen curiously. Ellen seemed to Barry to be about the same age as her own mother, or maybe a little younger. She had heavy blond hair pulled back into a big knot at the back, and her eyes were friendly and warm. She looked tired, Barry thought—tired and perhaps a little unhappy. There was something about her that made Barry feel sorry for her.

"You'd hardly know the place, would you?" Milly chattered on happily from across the room. "The town either, for that matter. Why, I can remember when I first came here there wasn't another building on Main Street besides the one your pa's business is in, Barry, and Miller's store. This restaurant wasn't here then, nor the drugstore. Just the one church and a couple of houses— the Goulds' and that other one——"

Alicia and Barry were looking at Milly politely. She talked and hung curtains and still managed to look over her shoulder at them now and then, so they felt it would be rude to look away, although neither of them was very much interested in what she said. They weren't watching Ellen, the new waitress, but looked around when she dropped one of their cokes with a crash.

"Never mind, Ellen; we've got lots of glasses," Milly said cheerfully, her round face beaming. "Don't think another thing about it."

Ellen hastily brushed the broken glass into a dust pan and with an apology for the delay, poured another glass of coke.

"I didn't know you'd been here that long," she said to Milly, when the cousins were busy with their drinks. "I thought you said you'd been here only about five years."

"That's right. I started this place five years ago, when I came back. I lived here for six years before, though, when I was first married. Bert and I tried farming his folks' place for a while, but he wasn't cut out to be a farmer and I guess I wasn't meant to be

a farmer's wife either. We left here and went down to Connecticut for a spell. We worked in a restaurant there. Then after he died, I got the idea of coming back here and opening up a lunchroom. Always did kind of like the town, and I didn't have any place else to go. Really wanted a big place, but this—oh, well."

Milly turned and looked at Ellen, who was just standing there, nervously wiping her hands on a towel.

"Ellen's just come here to work for me," Milly explained. "I needed more than just the one girl. We haven't had time to get acquainted yet, but we will. Pretty soon we'll know all there is to know about each other, won't we, Ellen—couple of women cooped up together all the time!"

Barry happened to be staring at Ellen's pale face as Milly spoke, and she saw a strange expression cross the thin features. Why, she's angry, she thought. Something Milly said made her mad! I wonder what it could have been? Was it Milly saying she'd get to know all about her? But that doesn't make sense. Just the same, Ellen's afraid of something. Afraid of what Milly will find out? What could Ellen possibly have to hide?

Chapter 6

Chris
Backs Out

The cousins and Chris were sitting at the edge of Minnow Brook on the smooth round rocks that were scattered there as though by a giant hand. The water was shallow at any time, but this year, because of long weeks with no rain, the creek had become just a trickle, not really deep enough for splashing even. Rusty, who still enjoyed rolling around in the inch or so of water, had led the girls to the spot, and Chris had appeared unexpectedly from the direction of the Bassetts'.

"The Bassetts went to Bedford early this morning," he said, "and won't be back until late this evening." He stretched happily. "A whole day off," he added. "Got my chores all done before ten o'clock."

"Then this is the perfect day for you to go to the Parrish place," Alicia told him sharply. "Go ahead, Chris. You always say you can't get away."

Chris looked at her lazily, chewing on a blade of grass. "What's your hurry?" he asked.

"Hurry! It's been a whole week since we asked you to go. And I'm only going to be here until Labor Day, you know."

Chris turned his back, and started to throw pebbles at a slowly drifting stick, and Barry and Alicia, after exchanging exasperated glances, began to discuss the new people in town. They had just discovered that the handsome Mr. Kenyon was a writer, but Alicia much preferred her own theory that he was a private detective or a secret agent.

"Why would anyone come to Northville to finish a book?" she said scornfully.

"It is pretty funny," Barry agreed. "And that waitress, that Ellen somebody. She's even funnier. There's something very strange about her. She's hiding something, I'm sure of it."

"Look, you two. If you've got any brains at all, you'll stop poking your silly noses into everybody's business," Chris called over his shoulder. "Stick to your crocheting or playing with dolls or whatever it is you like to do. Stop making up stories about people. What would she have to hide? Girls!" He snorted, and standing up suddenly, he crashed away through the bushes.

"Well, I never!" Alicia gasped. "Why did he get so cross, all of a sudden?" She giggled. "We've always been girls!"

Barry was troubled. There was more to Chris's anger than just being annoyed with them because they were girls. He had been really upset.

"I guess that proves it," she said quietly. "Chris *is* mixed up in all of this somehow. You were right."

Instead of looking triumphant, as Barry expected, Alicia nodded sadly. "And now we've made him mad. So I guess he'll never go and look around for us, will he?"

Barry shook her head glumly. "Not unless—— No, he won't," she said.

"Then I'll have to go," Alicia said darkly. "I never promised not to, you know."

Barry shook her head again. "You know you're not supposed to do anything I'm not allowed to do."

"Yes, I know. But—well, I have to go, don't I?"

Barry was torn. She wanted desperately to have someone visit the mysterious Parrish place, because she was sure that the key to the secret was there somehow, but she knew that if Alicia were caught and Barry's parents found out, she would suffer just as much as Alicia would.

"I'll just go, and your family won't know a thing about it," Alicia promised her, but her eyes were dark with excitement—and perhaps fear. "I've got to do it. Come on, let's go out to the road and get some cones or something at Miller's, just in case your father sees us go by. Then we could sort of wander out the road toward the river, where they're still working. That would look all right. Then we can cut across through the woods to the fence, down by the river somewhere. You can stand watch, and I—I'll climb over or through or something."

Barry looked at her cousin with new respect. She was sure that Alicia was frightened at the very idea of what she planned to do, but still she was willing to try it.

"OK," Barry said quietly. "Let's go."

The first part of the scheme was easy enough to carry out, and they reached the construction on the northbound road beyond the new cloverleaf before they had finished their ice-cream cones.

"Let's just pretend we haven't anything to do, and kind of wander around," Alicia suggested. "Gee, why didn't we bring Rusty?"

Barry understood. Alicia wasn't too fond of the Irish setter, and was forever fussing about the way he got wet or was always covered with dust or sand, so after his bath in the creek, Barry had sent him home. But at the moment Alicia saw in Rusty a protector of sorts.

"Let's go back and get him," Barry suggested.

"Oh, no, not when we've come this far." Alicia shook her head stubbornly. "Look, Barry, there's a kind of path. Let's take it. It must go to the fence, doesn't it?"

"I think so." In spite of herself, Barry felt nervous. There's not a thing in the world the matter with walking along this path, she scolded herself. I must be getting jumpy.

The faint track led them through trees and tangled thickets. As they left the work area, the sound of the machinery became a dull drone no louder than the constant hum and buzz of the bees and other insects around them. Unconsciously, the girls began to walk silently, almost on tiptoe, looking around fearfully, jumping slightly at the sound of a snapping twig, the sudden movement of a branch, or the deepening of a shadow.

"Spooky," Alicia whispered, and Barry nodded. Just ahead she had spied the links of the high metal fence, a gray web spread across their path and fading away through the trees. To the left, the fence led to the main gate. To the right was the river and somewhere, before they reached the river bank itself, there was the big fallen tree trunk that the boys had used to help them climb over the fence. If they found it, would Alicia be able to get over it too? Should she help Alicia? If she did, wouldn't that be every bit as bad, in the eyes of her parents, as climbing over herself?

Reluctantly, Barry turned to the right, her mind seething with mixed emotions. It was exciting to be here, and she wondered why she'd never come before. But it was also scary, even with Alicia along.

Although the path they had been following had been barred by the fence, there was a faint trail threading along the fence itself, which meant that a good many others had been interested in looking around here too. Barry started to whisper this thought to Alicia, but at that moment felt her cousin clutch her hand tightly.

"The tree," Barry whispered, seeing the dark shape for the first time. "There's——"

Alicia's fingers tightened on Barry's wrist and she shook her head. Barry heard the noise then. Footsteps, she decided, and was sure there had been a low murmur of voices too. She looked at her cousin in panic. Who could be there? Barry stood irresolutely, until she felt herself pulled back along the path by Alicia.

"Come on," Alicia urged under her breath. "It could be—anybody. Hurry!"

Suddenly Barry's mind began to work again. She seized Alicia's belt with her free hand and brought to a stop their headlong flight. Then, walking with elaborate care, she pulled Alicia off the path to a spot behind a big boulder.

"We've got to find out who it is," she whispered.

"But it might be somebody awful—somebody who'd kill us just for being here."

"Don't be silly," Barry whispered back, with a confidence she was far from feeling. "It's someone who's here for the same reason we are. And if we find out who it is, we might find out something we need to know."

Alicia looked at her cousin with open admiration. Then she nodded, and with a little shrug accepted Barry's leadership. In spite of her nervousness, Barry felt a thrill of pride. It had always been Alicia who'd been the boss. Perhaps it was her turn now!

They sat in silence, crouched behind the boulder and waiting for what seemed a very long time. The footsteps went away, and there was no sound of voices at all. Barry tried cautiously to shift her position, but Alicia shook her head warningly and Barry realized that if she moved, she could be seen from the path, so she let her cramped arms and legs resume their uncomfortable crouch. Just as she had decided she couldn't bear it another minute, she

felt Alicia's fingers tighten on her arm. Alicia, she thought, must have sharper ears, but a split second later she heard the sound of footsteps herself. Whoever it was wasn't making much effort to be quiet. She craned her neck as much as she dared, and caught a glimpse of a moving figure far away through the trees.

"Well, OK," she heard a low voice call, and she stared at Alicia with amazement.

"Chris?" Alicia mouthed silently, and Barry first nodded, then shook her head. She wasn't sure. He had popped into her mind too, but the low, almost whispered voice, told her nothing. They could hear one person crashing away through the bushes back of them, toward the river, and at the same time, there were light footsteps hurrying along the path they had just left. Alicia again seized Barry's arm convulsively, pulling her down beside her. The girls held their breath and squeezed their eyes tightly shut as the footsteps, light and hurried, went by on the path. Then Barry shook off Alicia's grasp. We must see who it is, she told herself firmly. With difficulty she straightened up, her bent knees protesting as she moved them from the position they had held too long. She pushed her head up cautiously.

"Can you see?" Alicia whispered. "Who is it? Do be careful!"

Barry nodded. She could see the retreating back clearly enough. Then she wheeled to stare in the opposite direction, catching a flash of blue moving through the trees.

"Who was it?" Alicia asked. "Do we know him?"

"It wasn't a him, it was a her. It was that waitress at Milly's."

"Oh, no! But why would she be with Chris?"

"It wasn't Chris," Barry said. "I distinctly saw that whoever it was was wearing a blue shirt, and Chris always wears white ones. Now, who wears blue shirts all the time? I know—that Roy Upton!"

"Yes, he does. But half the men you see on Main Street wear blue shirts," Alicia said, dusting grass and twigs from her bare knees. "Everybody *but* Chris." She sighed and added, "And now we've got to go back to that tree trunk and get me over the fence."

"No. That's out," Barry said firmly. "Come on, let's go home, Alicia. We'll have to think of something else."

Later Barry told herself that at the very moment when she had forced Alicia off the path and made her crouch behind the boulder, they had changed places. Now she was the one who made the suggestions and gave the orders, and Alicia, oddly enough, followed her mutely, agreed with what she said, never objecting or complaining. Barry liked this new arrangement; it gave her a heady feeling of leadership.

The day after their thwarted attempt to get into the Parrish estate, the cousins were jolted by an unexpected bit of news.

"Just as we thought," Barry's father was saying to his wife as the girls wandered out near the porch, their hands full of freshly baked chocolate cookies. "The new roads are bringing in all sorts of undesirable characters. Not to mention the publicity, of course." Barry gave Alicia a warning look and they stopped in their tracks. "That kid at the filling station—he's a wrong one, I guess," Mr. Loomis went on. "Bernie Jones caught him shinnying over the fence, or trying to maybe, out at the Parrish house. You know how Bernie feels about that. When they made him the town one-man police force, he said that was one thing he was going to see to—that nobody ever got in there and broke windows and things the way they do to empty houses. He told me he's appointing a couple of deputies to help him keep an eye on the place. For a while, anyway."

"I don't like that young man's looks much," Mrs. Loomis observed.

"No. He's not the kind of character we want around this town. Not much we can do about it, I guess. Bernie said he'd make life as unpleasant for him as possible, but the boy may have a thick skin. He looks it. Bernie says he figures the kid's spent a lot of time out there in the last few weeks, looking the place over. There's a kind of pathway along the fence that Bernie said was so overgrown you could hardly see it a month ago, but now it's an honest-to-goodness trail almost all the way down to the river."

Barry and Alicia stared at one another with round eyes.

"I wonder," Mrs. Loomis mused, "if that old place doesn't just draw people to it naturally."

"Because it's empty?" her husband asked.

"No. Well, maybe that too. But—you know, because of its history. Lots of people in town must have been there to stare at the place at one time or another, and if the new people in town have heard the story, then naturally they'll be attracted to it too."

Barry frowned at Alicia, thinking, I bet we could go right out there on the porch and make my parents tell us what this is all about. She swallowed the last of the cookie she'd been chewing and squared her shoulders, only to hear her father say, "I hope the girls don't ever hear anything about it all. They're just the age to be a little too curious."

"I'm glad they're girls." Mrs. Loomis laughed. "Boys would be a handful right now."

Barry flashed Alicia a smile, and almost choked at the face Alicia made in return. Wordlessly, they tiptoed back to the kitchen.

"We'll never find out anything," Alicia complained in a low voice. "I wish we *were* boys."

"So do I. Well, come on," Barry said, banging the cover of the cookie tin as loudly as possible, and they scuffed and stamped their feet noisily as they went to join Mr. and Mrs. Loomis on the porch.

Chapter 7

Alicia
Decides

On their next trip to the "off-limits" property, Barry and Alicia walked along on the other side of the gate and toward the far side of the house. Here the going was more difficult because there was no track whatever for them to follow, and the woods were even more dense.

"There's nothing to see on this side," Alicia announced, looking with distaste at the long scratches that marred the smooth tan of her legs. "Just a couple of little buildings that are caving in, and the chimney that fell down all over that funny looking oven where they used to make bricks."

"There's nothing to see on the other side either," Barry pointed out. "And you know we shouldn't be here anyway!" Sometimes she felt as though they were wasting Alicia's whole visit—and this was the start of the third week of her stay. By now they should have made several trips to the lake, among other things.

I'm supposed to be the leader now, she told herself. And I'm going to stop this silly business. She glanced at Alicia and said aloud, "You know what I want? A nice big ice-cream soda. Rusty will wait for us outside of the store. I'll treat. Come on." That, she thought, should forestall any suggestion that they plod around the fence again.

Alicia brightened up at once. "Wonderful," she said. "And Mr. Farrell makes such super-dupers."

Barry looked at her cousin in surprise. It was the first time she'd heard any praise from Alicia about the sodas at Farrell's Drug Store. Instead there was usually a hymn of praise for the Jolly Jumbo Sodas at an ice-cream store in Bedford. Barry was still shaking her head over it as she led the way into the cool fragrance of the drugstore.

"Hi, Mr. Farrell," she said, climbing up on a stool. "A strawberry ice-cream soda with strawberry ice cream, please."

"Me, too." Alicia climbed up beside Barry. They watched with interest as Mr. Farrell made the sodas. Just as he put them, pink and frothing, in front of the girls, the telephone rang at the back of the store. He pushed the container of straws closer to them and hurried away.

"Two scoops of ice cream," Alicia whispered. "Did you notice? My, these are good!"

When the sodas were half gone, Barry began to look around. There was a newspaper lying on the counter beside her, and she glanced at it idly. It was not the *Bedford Courier*, which was delivered to the Loomis mailbox each day, but one from a city in another state. The date on it, she saw, was almost six months before. Written across the white margin at the top was *"See p. 16"* in a pencilled scrawl.

Barry was curious. Mr. Farrell was back in his little prescription room, still talking on the telephone and looking through his shelves, carrying the phone with him as he evidently searched for something the person on the other end of the line must be asking for. There was nothing wrong, she figured, in looking at someone else's newspaper anyway—especially one left carelessly on a drugstore counter. She picked up the folded paper and carefully opened it to page sixteen, where her eye immediately fell on a pencilled circle around a news item that was only about three inches long. Idly, still, Barry began to read, but before long she gasped.

"What's the matter?" Alicia asked, more interested in dislodging a piece of strawberry that had wedged itself into her straw than in the answer to her question.

Barry frowned and read on hurriedly. "Alicia, look!" she whispered, with one more glance at Mr. Farrell's white-coated back. "Quick, before he gets through in there."

Together they read the item: "Mr. and Mrs. Sidney Marble have sold their house on West Green Street and are moving to Northville, where they plan to open the Marble Motel, now building, at the junction of the new routes 118 and 17. The Marbles have managed the Star Bright Motel and Restaurant in this city for the last six years, and before that were employed by hotels in Texas and Tennessee.

"Mr. Marble, in an interview, pointed out that Northville was the subject of a syndicated story, published recently, on a colorful era in its past history, when gold was smuggled from Canada through the quiet little town. Periodically rumors of a cache of gold, buried in haste to keep government agents from discovering it, have been spread about, luring treasure hunters to the area. 'Whether or not there is any truth in those rumors, it is not possible to say,' Mr. Marble commented, 'but it is known that the smuggled gold, real or imagined, has cost more than one life.'

"Perhaps the new prominence of Northville, thanks to the ambitious new highway program, will revive interest in Northville's past and its presumed treasure."

The two girls stared at each other wordlessly. With a quick look at Mr. Farrell, Alicia picked up the newspaper, folded it, and handed it to Barry, who put it back in its place on the counter. When Mr. Farrell at last returned from his telephone conversation, the girls were sucking busily on their straws.

Barry dug into her pocket, pulled out the dollar bill she had buttoned in there before they left home that morning, gave it to Mr. Farrell, and impatiently waited for her change.

"Thank you, Mr. Farrell," Alicia said sweetly. "That was the best strawberry ice-cream soda I've ever had in my whole life."

Mr. Farrell looked pleased, if slightly startled, and the cousins scuttled out of the drug store into the bright sun.

"Oh, Barry!" Alicia cried. "I can hardly stand it. Gold! Buried treasure! Imagine!"

"Shh." Barry looked around cautiously. "Everybody's worked so hard to keep us from hearing about it, I guess we'd better not let them find out we know. That business about it 'costing more than one life' has to mean that Mr. Parrish and Uncle Louis. And probably that's why they put a fence around the Parrish house. Just supposing we hadn't gone in there for sodas! Or that paper hadn't been left on the counter! What we would have missed!"

Alicia's mind appeared to be working busily, because she nodded absently and said, "Now we've *got* to go to the Parrish place again and look for the gold."

Barry scowled. "We shouldn't go there and you know it," she said severely. "So forget it, Alicia. I'm going to the creek."

Alicia flashed Barry a furious look. "When we could be finding oodles and oodles of gold and be rich! Not me."

"Then you go ahead and look."

"All right, I will. I don't understand you, Barry! You were just as excited as I was, a minute ago. Well, I'll find it and then you'll be sorry."

Barry looked after Alicia's straight little figure in despair. "She won't get very far," she muttered at last. "She hates being in the woods alone. She'll think up some excuse and come tearing back. Come on, Rusty, let's go get cooled off."

For the second time, Barry found herself at the creek without Alicia. For a while she was angry with her cousin, but the anger turned to jealousy. Supposing she does get over the fence, she thought in despair. How she'll crow! And if she finds those gold pieces—she'll be unbearable!

All at once the creek stopped being fun, the sky appeared to darken, and the faint breeze freshened uncomfortably.

"Let's go, Rusty. And don't look at me like that. I don't know what's wrong with me today either!"

She began to dry herself hastily with the towel she had brought, but before she finished there was the sound of running feet.

"It's Alicia," she said to the setter. "Isn't it, Rusty?" His plumed tail wagged the answer, and they waited.

When Alicia appeared, her face was red from running, and she was too out of breath to talk. Barry sat down on a rock and fidgeted impatiently. Finally Alicia kicked off her canvas shoes and plunged her feet into the cool water.

"Oh, that feels good," she exclaimed gratefully. "You don't know what I've been through. I was chased by a wolf or—or something horrible."

"Don't be silly. There aren't any wolves around here," Barry scoffed.

"Well, a big dog maybe. Or a bear. But I still think it was a wolf." Alicia shuddered. "Wait till I tell you. I went along the fence—I was going to find that tree, you know, and figure out a way to get over."

"You can't do that alone."

"I was going to *try*," Alicia said with dignity. "And I got quite a way along when I heard a—a noise." She looked at Barry apologetically and added, "I was scared blue. Honest. Then I thought it must be one of the deputies Bernie Jones has keeping an eye on the place. Then all of a sudden I heard panting. This wolf or bear, or whatever it was, began to pant. Like this."

Rusty looked at Alicia, who was pretending to pant frantically, with such curiosity that Barry burst into a fit of giggles.

"I'm sure bears don't pant. I don't know about wolves."

"They're kind of like dogs, aren't they? Well anyway, I could hear this panting, and a lot of cracking and sort of stamping and running like, and it was growing nearer. Oh," she finished, making a face, "did I run!"

"I would have run too," Barry said.

"Next time I'll take Rusty."

"Next time! Alicia Loomis, you're not going back there ever again."

"Yes, I am," Alicia said stubbornly. "But with Rusty."

Barry sighed. "And with me too, I guess," she said sadly.

Alicia's troubled face cleared. "That's wonderful," she said with relief. "I won't mind, if you're there."

She dabbled her feet silently for a moment, then stretched out a hand for Barry's towel. "I can't stand it!" she exclaimed suddenly. "It's only three more days until my family comes, and then on Monday we leave. Just when everything's getting so exciting. I can't bear it!"

Alicia was strangely quiet as they walked back to the house. Barry, thinking about her cousin's departure, realized that it wouldn't be nearly as much fun looking for gold by herself. Still, when she did find it, she would be rich and get her picture in all the papers.

"Barry Loomis finds long-lost treasure!" She could see the headlines now. "Twelve-year-old Northville girl solves old mystery!" "Loomis family buys mansion once home of wealthy Parrish family." Barry's head fairly swam with headlines, all of them exciting.

When they reached the house, Alicia interrupted Barry's bliss-ful daydreams saying, "I'm going to call my father."

"Call him! But he's going to be here on Saturday! What do you want to talk to him about?"

"You'll see," Alicia said, turning back to the porch where Barry had stopped for a moment. "No, I guess I'd better tell you first. Before Aunt Ann gets home too. You see, Barry, there was some-thing I never told you."

"You're a clam," Barry said with a grin. "You knew about the 'old trouble,' and you never mentioned it to me. And now an-other secret?"

"This is different. It's about me. Sit down in the swing, and I'll tell you. You see, for a long time—ever since last Christmas, after you left our place—Daddy's been trying to sell me on the idea of coming here to live with you."

"Live with us? All of you?" Barry was astonished.

"No, just me. You see, Daddy wants to go to Europe to see about making some kind of arrangements for the factory. I don't understand it, exactly, but I guess he thinks he can get some of the things made, or partly made, cheaper over there. Anyway, he and Mother thought they'd go over and spend a couple of months —maybe longer—but they couldn't go during the summer for some reason, and there isn't anybody they could get to stay with me for so long."

"Why don't you go with them?"

"Oh, Barry, don't you want me here?"

"Sure, Alicia. I didn't mean that," Barry said hastily. "I just thought—well, wouldn't you want to go to Europe?"

"I don't know. I guess so. But anyway, they said I couldn't miss school for that long." Alicia made a face. "So their idea was for me to come here for a year. They're building a new junior high right near us, but it won't be ready for a whole year, and the old school is awfully crowded, with double sessions and all that.

Daddy and Mother figured I could go to school here with you for this one year, and they could go to Germany and all those other places, and everything would be just peachy."

"Well, it would," Barry exclaimed. "What fun, Alicia!"

"Yes. The only trouble is—I refused," Alicia said with an embarrassed smile. "I'm sorry, Barry, but I couldn't see it for dust. I said I didn't want to live in this—this——"

"Whistle stop?"

"Yes. I made an awful fuss. Finally Mother said they wouldn't make me if I felt so bad about it, and maybe Daddy would go without her. But nothing was settled when I left."

"Do my folks know about it?" Barry asked curiously. I must be awful easy to keep secrets from, she thought, because they must know. And they never let on.

"Of course. Daddy said they were all for it. You wouldn't mind, Barry, if I came here to live?"

"I think it would be just super!" Even as the words spilled out of her, Barry realized that if she had been asked three weeks before if Alicia could live in Northville for a year, she wouldn't have been very enthusiastic about the idea. Come to think of it, once or twice her father had asked her if she wouldn't like Alicia to stay longer. She had thought he was just teasing her. "Go ahead and telephone your father. Or your mother."

"I'd rather talk to Daddy. He doesn't—fuss so. No, you stay here, please. I'd rather talk to Daddy alone."

Barry knew why. Alicia would have to take back some uncomplimentary remarks about Northville. No wonder she wanted to be alone!

Only five minutes later, Alicia came running out on the porch, her face beaming. "Daddy says he's tickled pink. I guess they were going to try to convince me this weekend anyway. He's going to have the movers come next week and pick up my whole bedroom set. He said there's room here for all of it. Is there, Barry?"

"Of course. My old nursery is miles bigger than your room in Bedford. Oh, that's why they had it all done over!"

"And Daddy says they'll bring the clothes I'll need for starting school when they come on Saturday. Oh, here comes your mother. Aunt Ann, Aunt Ann, I'm coming to live with you— wait till you hear!"

Alicia tumbled down the steps of the porch and ran to Mrs. Loomis. Barry, watching, began to wonder. It had seemed a wonderful idea, at first. But what would it do to her friendships with the girls and boys she had always known in Northville? She sighed. Then she remembered something—the gold, the smuggled gold. The mystery. That was the most important thing of all, just now, and with Alicia on hand she was sure they could solve it. Alone, she was just a twelve-year-old girl wandering around aimlessly, but with Alicia she could develop a plan of action.

"Well, Barry, how do you feel about having a sister for a year?"

Barry turned and smiled at her mother. "Wonderful," she said enthusiastically.

"But what happened to change your mind, Alicia?"

Alicia smiled at her aunt, her brown eyes clear and innocent. Barry took a deep breath. She was glad that Alicia too felt it was important not to let Barry's parents know just why she had suddenly decided to stay in Northville. Otherwise they'd be watched closely, Barry knew, and given a lot of instructions about what not to do and places not to visit.

"I just did," Alicia said simply. "I like Northville now, Aunt Ann. It's—it's grown up, somehow. I like it here."

Chapter 8

Around
the Fence

"In my whole life," Barry said earnestly, "I have never known such confusion!"

"And in my whole life, neither have I," her father told her. "And I've lived about three times as long as you have, remember."

It was true that from the moment of Alicia's telephone call to her father's office, things had happened fast. Alicia's parents arrived on Saturday with not only their usual supply of luggage, always large, but with extra bags and boxes full of Alicia's clothes and personal treasures. The two Mrs. Loomises spent most of the weekend discussing school clothes and making lists, while their husbands talked of nothing but politics or European methods of manufacture. Barry and Alicia were more or less free to come and go as they pleased, but they were afraid they'd miss something if they left home for too long.

"Besides," Alicia said practically, "they'll ask us sooner or later where we've been. With four of them, one of them is bound to. My folks will leave Monday, and we'll get back to normal."

"We'll get back to school soon after, though," Barry remarked gloomily. "And then there won't be much time for looking for—you know what."

"We'll make time," Alicia insisted. She loved being the center of so much excitement, Barry could tell, but she wasn't prepared for Alicia's reaction when her parents finally left. It was as though she realized for the first time that they were going far away and that she wouldn't see them for months and months—perhaps not until spring. She looked as though the world had come to an end.

"Your father has the chance of a lifetime to combine business with pleasure," Mr. Loomis told his niece gently. "I wish I had the same opportunity. And we're not so hard to get along with, even in big doses!"

Alicia brightened up for the first time when her bedroom furniture arrived. Her mother had sent along a huge amount of flowered cotton fabric which Barry's mother had Mrs. Atkins make up into curtains, a new bedspread, and a dressing table skirt, and Alicia was proud of her big, new room. Then school started, and Barry introduced her cousin to her own friends, most of whom hadn't seen Alicia before since she'd only been in Northville in the summer time.

At first the routine of school and homework left few spare moments for solving mysteries or for treasure-hunting. "And we'd better get going," Alicia commented darkly. "I probably wouldn't even be here, if it weren't for that. But it seems harder now."

"That's because there are so many people around," Barry told her. "All the kids are back and going to school. And the motel's partly open, with people living in it, and the new restaurant that's being built out on the Bedford Road has brought a whole new crew of workmen to town."

"And every time we go anywhere near the Parrish place—just going by on the highway—we see people there. Maybe they're only taking walks. But I don't think so," Alicia said frowning.

"I guess Bernie Jones doesn't think so either. They say his men are walking around the fence most of the time. We'll never get near it now."

Alicia nodded. Then she giggled. "What a dull job, just walking from one end of the fence to the other. Anyway, they'll make a path so we won't have so much trouble—Barry, what's the matter?"

"I just had an idea. That's it!"

"What's it?"

"I know how we can get to the house. It's the fence—it goes down to the river on either side." She saw the bewilderment on Alicia's face and explained. "The fence doesn't go along the front, by the river. Chris told me that. It just goes down on the sides and ends at the river. All we have to do is get beyond it, and there's nothing to stop us."

"You mean we could crawl by?"

"Or swim, maybe. Well, we couldn't do that, but we could get a boat and just row right up to the place."

"Your family won't let us."

"They won't know. And besides, what they always said was not to try to get through the fence or over it. You heard them the other day, when Daddy was telling you the rules," Barry said, trying to ease her conscience.

"They meant going to the house. If they knew about the fence ending, they would have said we shouldn't try to get there that way either."

"But they probably don't know. And if they do, they know we haven't a boat anyhow."

"We sure don't."

"I know," Barry said impatiently. "Well, we'll borrow one."

"Where?"

"I don't know yet. But I'll think about it. Anyway, now we know how we can get there."

"We can ask Chris to help."

"You and your one-track mind," Barry said crossly. "You know how Chris has been acting lately—as if we were poison. I'm not going to go running after him. And we don't need him; we can do this alone."

Now the mystery was important again, occupying their waking thoughts, and sometimes the girls dreamed about the gold, too. They decided that the first weekend in October, now that school work was more or less under control, would be the time when they would take their big step.

"I talked to Lester Graham," Barry reported. "He's awful, of course, but his father has two boats. They live right where the creek joins the river, you know, and they have a big dock. Daddy said it used to be a boathouse, for a big boat, but the river got too shallow or something. Anyway, Lester said I could borrow the rowboat. I told him you wanted to see the river," she added with a giggle. "So don't forget to look excited when we get there."

"Me!" squeaked Alicia. "I don't even want to get into his old boat. And I can't stand Lester Graham. Why me?"

"It would look kind of funny if all of a sudden I decided I just had to row along North River, wouldn't it? After living here all these years?"

"I suppose so. If you ask me, it's kind of funny he'd let us have his boat anyway."

"I—I kind of promised to ask him to my birthday party," Barry admitted. "Well, I *had* to do something. He's always tried to get friendly and I kind of freeze him out." She sighed. "Now I suppose he'll think we're buddies. And he goes for you, Alicia, I can tell."

Alicia shuddered. Lester Graham was fat, and he had fine

baby hair that looked funny above his pale, round face. He had no friends in town, and because he lived nearer to Barry than anyone else her age—until Chris moved in with the Bassetts anyway—he had been a problem for as long as Barry could remember. Now she had reopened the case, and knew it, but Lester's boat was the only one she could think of.

"He wanted to row us," she added. "I had to persuade him I was pretty good at rowing myself. Imagine having that drip along!"

Barry had arranged with Lester to borrow the boat on Saturday afternoon, and the girls discovered then that Barry hadn't been quite as persuasive as she'd hoped.

"My pop doesn't like having strangers take his boats on the river," Lester said, his little eyes gleaming in his pudgy face. "So I'll go with you."

"Lester Graham, you promised," Barry stormed, throwing an agonized look at her cousin. Alicia at once came to the rescue.

"Oh, Lester, please," she cooed sweetly. "Barry is a wonderful rower, really. My Uncle George taught her. And this is a private expedition, you see. It's a kind of a secret—we're cousins, you know, and we've planned it for a long time. So we just have to go alone, Lester."

Lester looked puzzled, but he gave in to Alicia's wheedling voice. The girls scrambled into the rowboat, and Barry, embarrassed at having an audience, first had trouble getting the oars into the oarlocks and then caught a crab on her very first pull. But she managed finally to get the boat out into the middle of the river where the current helped to move them along.

"Don't forget you'll be rowing upstream coming home," Lester called after her anxiously. "Sure you can do it?"

"I'm sure," Barry shouted back and pulled vigorously. Actually she was quite at home in a boat, for the Loomises had had one until the year before when the depth of Minnow Brook was changed by some damming upstream and her father had said the boat was now useless to them. "What were you talking about?" she asked Alicia, when the boat was nicely under way. "What has our being cousins got to do with it?"

Alicia giggled. "Nothing. I had to say something, didn't I? It worked anyway."

Barry began to watch the shore as she let the boat more or less drift along, giving an occasional pull to keep them in midchannel and to help their speed a bit. For the first time she realized what a long, hard row back it would be against the current. She wondered if perhaps she shouldn't have accepted Lester's offer, but the thought of having him along on their adventure was distasteful, and there would be no way to get rid of him when they reached their destination.

Alicia was also staring at the river bank, but in a more carefree manner. Beyond the Graham's dock, where Minnow Brook flowed into North River, the shoreline was less thickly wooded. Across the fields they could see the spires of the two churches, and a tiny flag fluttered above the old building that was Miller's store.

"Gee, things look different," Alicia said. "Did you ever come down this far before? On the river, I mean."

"Oh, sure," Barry said airily. "Hundreds of times." With Daddy rowing, she added to herself.

"How far? As far as we're going?"

"No," Barry said. "We only went as far as the old bridge."

"The bridge!" exclaimed Alicia. "Supposing someone sees us from the bridge! Cars are using it now, remember?"

Barry bit her lip. The old stone bridge with the curved arch, which people were always taking pictures of, had been pulled down and a new cement bridge, four lanes wide, had been built in its place. "I don't think you can see anything on the river from the cars," she said. "Remember the day we went to look at the new bridge? It had walls on both sides."

Barry hated to admit even to herself that she had completely forgotten about the bridge. Although she had never been told not to borrow a boat and row on the river, she felt her father wouldn't approve. If they were seen, she wouldn't mind owning up later, but supposing some friend of her father's—or even her father himself—should see the boat now and stop them from completing their mission!

"There's the bridge!" Alicia cried. She had the advantage, of course, of facing toward the bow of the boat, while Barry had to turn around in her seat and crane. "And it's OK. I can only see the tops of the cars. So no one can see us."

Barry began to row in earnest. They moved swiftly down the river, floated under the bridge, listening to the thunder of the cars as they passed overhead, and went around a gentle bend in the river.

"There it is!" Alicia breathed. "Oh, isn't it huge! Look, Barry, there's a dock there—sort of like the one at Lester's. There's even a boathouse at the end, except it looks kind of caved in. Oh do hurry. I'm so excited!"

Barry rowed toward the river's edge as fast as she could. At first she tried to bring the boat alongside the dock, but the current made that difficult. "The dock's no good anyhow," she said, looking at its rotting boards with distaste. "I'll pull up on the sand."

They beached the boat and pulled it up carefully. "If it floats away, we'll never get home," Barry said sternly. "One more yank, Alicia." She even took the precaution of tying the painter around a stake she saw at the edge of the sand. The little green rowboat, she felt, represented their only hope of getting away from the place and back to their own world.

Alicia, usually timid wandering around outdoors and inclined to jump at the smallest sound, darted across the unkempt lawn in front of the big gray house and hurried from one window to another, cupping her hands at her temples so that she could peer inside. "The furniture is all there, but it's covered up with sheets or something," she reported. "I can't budge these windows. Maybe around back."

Barry followed her cousin slowly. Now that they were here, she began to worry. Such a risk to take—and for what?

Alicia dashed ahead happily. In a few minutes they had gone all the way around the big, square house and had peeked into all of the windows that could be reached from the ground or from the porches.

"I thought it would be much more—well, scary," Alicia confessed. "It isn't a bit. And I don't see anything, do you?"

Barry shook her head. "What did you expect to see? I don't even know why we're here, really."

"Don't be silly. We've got to keep looking." Alicia's bright eyes darted around curiously. "I know—let's go down to the boathouse."

"Be careful!" Barry warned. "The old dock is full of holes." She teetered after Alicia, setting her feet carefully on the worn and splintered boards. Alicia reached the boathouse long before Barry did, and as she approached, Alicia turned a white face.

"Barry, look! Somebody must be living here."

Her heart fluttering, Barry peered through the cracked window. The dark water, moving restlessly in the open space in the middle of the ramshackle building, made an eerie light that played about on the broken walls. An occasional shaft of sunlight probed through the partly ruined roof. As her eyes grew accustomed to the weird light, she saw that there was a cot pulled up against the far wall, under a window which was almost entirely covered by a length of dark material. An old khaki blanket was

tossed carelessly on the bottom of the canvas cot, and a light shirt hung limply on a nail just above it.

"Is that shirt blue?" Barry whispered. "It must be that—well, whoever it was we saw with the waitress that day. And whoever it is lives here in the boathouse. Let's go."

"There isn't anyone here now," Alicia retorted. "And it's broad daylight, so what are you scared of?"

"I'm not scared but—let's go home."

"No. Now that we finally got here, we've got to look around. Don't be such a baby. That stuff may have been here for years, you know."

Barry eyed Alicia suspiciously. Wasn't she talking just a little too loudly? Perhaps she was just as scared. "Well, all right. But let's hurry. I don't like it here."

Alicia walked carefully until she reached the end of the dock. Then she dashed across the lawn again. "We didn't look anywhere but right into the house itself," she said, as Barry caught up with her. "Let's go back to where that old shed is. We might even find a way to get back to the brickyard. Then we can go."

Barry followed reluctantly. Little as she liked this expedition, she felt she'd rather be with Alicia than by herself. Alicia suddenly stopped so short that Barry bumped into her.

"Look." Alicia pointed to the ground. "Footprints! And that's mud—it hasn't even dried from the rain last night, so somebody——"

"Somebody's here right now!" Barry whispered fiercely. "Come on, Alicia."

Alicia needed no urging. The two girls turned and fled along the shadows beside the house and emerged thankfully into the sunlight beyond. Wordlessly they ran down the sloping lawn, tripping over tall grass and tangled weeds, hurrying as fast as they could. This time it was Barry who was in the lead, and this time it was Barry who stopped short in her tracks.

"The boat!" she cried, in a strange voice that was halfway between a whisper and a scream. "Oh, Alicia, the boat's gone! What'll we do now?"

Chapter 9

The Long Road Home

The world had never seemed so large or so full of shadows and strange, lurking creatures. Barry, staring at the deep groove in the sand that marked the spot where Lester Graham's boat had been, decided that she and Alicia had wandered into a bad dream. She looked at her cousin and saw that she must be thinking much the same thing. "Never mind, Alicia, we'll get out of it somehow," she said, trying to sound much more confident than she felt.

"But, Barry," Alicia whispered, "that proves there's somebody here. He just came and stole our boat. He might be—anywhere."

Both girls looked fearfully at the boathouse, remembering the cot, the carelessly tossed khaki blanket, the shirt hanging on a nail.

"The door to the boathouse—the water part, I mean, where the boat is supposed to go in—was closed. And I bet it hasn't been open for years," Barry said in a very low voice. "But maybe he put the rowboat in there. Should we look?"

"Maybe it just drifted away by itself," Alicia suggested weakly.

"You know it couldn't have done that. Remember how far we pulled it up? I even tied it. And this is a river—no high or low tides." Barry wished she couldn't find so many reasons for proving Alicia wrong. But worst of all was standing there with the feeling that someone could be watching them, right this minute.

"What'll we do, Barry?"

"Let's—get out of here," Barry decided. "Come on, take your shoes and socks off. We can wade to the fence and then walk around it, and go out to the road on the other side. We know the path comes most of the way to the river anyway. Maybe all the way."

Alicia sat down beside Barry and pulled her shoes off obediently, looking over her shoulder as though she expected someone or something to jump at her. Barry felt the same way. She picked up her shoes, stretched out a free hand to Alicia, and said, "Come on. The sooner we get out of here the better."

Alicia seized her hand gratefully, and Barry was glad to have the cold fingers to hang onto, but as soon as they reached the water, they were forced to let go. The narrow sandy beach, so flat above the waterline, sloped down sharply under the water. Barry took a deep breath and stepped forward cautiously. The water was icy cold!

"It's freezing," Alicia complained, drawing back.

"Of course it is. It's October. Come on," Barry snapped. But the third tiny step took her up to her knees. "It's deep here," she wailed. "One more step and I bet it'd be over our heads. It's too cold to swim, and we couldn't go all the way home soaking wet. We've just got to go back, Alicia."

Back on land, Alicia rubbed her cold, wet feet with her socks and regarded Barry fearfully. "Now what'll we do?" she wailed.

"Well," began Barry, "there's only one thing to do, I guess. We'll have to climb over the fence. No one ever said anything against climbing *out* over the fence," she added, brightening. "Did they?"

"Who cares?" Alicia said fretfully. "Just so we get out of here. This boat business was your idea—it's all your fault."

Barry looked at Alicia coldly. It didn't help any to realize that what her cousin said was true, but after all, Alicia had more or less goaded her into it. "It won't do us any good to fight about it," she said sadly. "And now we've got to go climb that fence."

They put on their shoes, looking around cautiously. Barry couldn't shake the uncomfortable feeling that someone was nearby, peering at them. She felt she really should go and look in the boathouse, but she lacked the courage. If anyone was there, she was sure she didn't want to walk along those broken boards just to look in at him.

"Come on," she said, trying to ignore the fact that her left shoe was filled with wet, gritty sand. "If we go back by the house on this side and keep close to the fence, we should come to where that fallen tree is, on the other side of the fence. If people come in that way, they probably go out there too."

Alicia followed again, muttering only, "It's dark here. I'm cold."

Barry was glad to get out of the patch of darkness that was the shadow of the big house, although the tangled growth ahead looked almost impossible to get through. Finally she thought she detected a slight path running parallel to the fence. It was even more faint than the one on the other side of the fence, but it had been walked over at one time and it would be the easiest way to get back through the underbrush. The trouble was, she thought, whoever had taken the boat might be on the path, or someone else might be. Since there was no trace of the boat along the river in front of the house, whoever took it must have rowed away in it. If she could only be sure there was only one person involved, even that would help.

Barry's thoughts were interrupted by Alicia, who seized her arm from behind and whispered, "Barry, look!"

Barry followed the direction of Alicia's pointing finger and frowned. "I don't see anyone."

"Look right between those two trees, the thin ones. See? It's like a little lake or something. Just beyond the fence."

Curiosity got the better of Barry's fear for the moment. Alicia, she thought grudgingly, had sharp eyes. She hadn't seen the patch of water at all. They stared at it quietly for a moment. It seemed to be a woodland pool, surrounded by rocky banks two or three feet high. The water was still and, because it was so well shaded by the stand of trees all around, could have been a sheet of dark glass.

"It's an awfully funny place for a lake," Alicia whispered. "Don't you think so?"

Barry nodded. Her eyes followed the rocky ridges that formed the banks of the pool, and she saw that although the water ended in a soft curve, the banks themselves did not. They ran, almost exactly parallel, right up to the fence and beyond.

"It's almost like a road," she said softly. "See, it comes right up here."

They were whispering out of habit, but their fear for the moment was forgotten. Both girls were fascinated by the glassy surface of the dark water, lying so quietly, hidden away in the woods.

"You know," Alicia said at last, "I bet that isn't a lake at all. It's part of the river."

"It couldn't be," Barry protested. "It—why yes, you could be right! Maybe the river comes all the way up here in the spring, when there's a lot of water in it."

"It looks as though someone had dug it out almost. Do you think they could have?"

"Maybe. Look, this isn't getting us out of here. Let's go, Alicia.

That's awfully funny though, that place. Maybe sometime we can come back and——"

"Come back? Not me! Never!"

Barry grinned, went back to the path, and began following it. The bare branches caught at her legs, and the snapping of dry twigs reminded her that they still had to be careful because, for all they knew, there was still someone around. Half of her mind was on the hidden pool. "Alicia," she murmured, "I'll bet that's where our boat is."

"Where?"

"In that—that ditch, or whatever it is. But down toward the river, where we couldn't see it."

"But how could we get to it?"

"Oh, we can't. I didn't mean that. But I bet that's where it is. Come *on*," Barry urged, "we must have been here for hours and hours."

They covered a few more yards. Barry, peering through the fence for some sign of the fallen tree that would somehow, she hoped, mean escape from this nightmare, felt her arm clutched by Alicia once more.

"Barry, I heard someone. Footsteps. I'm sure of it."

They clung together in terror. Barry wondered if they shouldn't run somewhere—but where? And she wasn't at all sure her legs would work.

"I see someone," Alicia breathed. Barry looked over her shoulder. She could see a dark figure through the trees now, and the sound of footsteps was unmistakable.

"Oh, of course!" she said in a low voice. "It's one of the men Bernie Jones has here. How could we have forgotten all about them? We didn't have to be so scared all this time. We could have just yelled, and they'd find us."

"They'll catch us trespassing."

"Who cares!" Barry breathed, and Alicia nodded. They faced

the approaching figure bravely. "Oh, it's that man who's staying at the Goulds'—Mr. Kenyon," Barry said. She felt strangely relieved, although she couldn't have said why. Mr. Kenyon was an unknown quantity; it would have been much better if it had been Bernie Jones or one of his deputies. But even though he was an unknown quantity, Barry thought it would be difficult to imagine him stealing a boat or sleeping in an old boathouse. But what was he doing here, inside the fence?

They stood still, waiting for the man to walk up to them.

"Well, you two, what are you doing here?" he asked, his blue eyes twinkling at them.

"We're trespassing." It was Alicia who found her voice first.

"For that matter, I guess I am, too." He smiled at her. "How did you get here? Over the fence?"

"We came on the river," Barry told him. "In a boat we borrowed. And somebody stole it."

"Stole your boat?" He looked at her sharply. "You mean just now?"

Barry nodded. "We left it on the shore."

"It didn't just drift away?"

"No, we pulled it way up and tied it. We were—walking around, and when we went back to get it, it was gone."

Mr. Kenyon looked down at them intently, staring first at one and then the other. "Show me," he said, and there was such authority in his voice that the girls turned and went back toward the river without another word.

"Can you show us how to get out?" Alicia asked. "We—well, we——"

"Yes, of course. Just as soon as we take a look around," he promised. From the expression on Alicia's face, Barry knew that her cousin trusted Mr. Kenyon just as she did herself.

Paul Kenyon carefully examined the mark of the boat's keel. "You pulled it up properly," he said solemnly. "So you're right—

someone took it. You girls wait here a minute." They watched him walk out onto the broken dock, picking his way carefully. He was very thin, Barry thought, but he was so tall he must weigh a lot more than she did, or Alicia. She hoped the rotted wood wouldn't give way under him.

Mr. Kenyon peered into the boathouse window for a moment, then returned. Barry thought he didn't seem in the least interested in the cot and the blanket and shirt. Perhaps they did belong to him after all, and he was just checking up.

"OK, let's go," he said cheerfully.

Alicia, who had been silent for a long time—for her—suddenly burst into conversation. "We think we know where the boat might be. There's a little lake all kind of tucked away in the woods, and we decided it goes into the river somehow, and whoever took our boat might have hidden it there."

"Why would you think that?" The man looked amused. "Why wouldn't he just row away in it. Was it a good boat?"

Barry nodded gloomily. "And we borrowed it, besides."

He laughed. "It isn't easy to hide a boat on a river as small as this one," he said. "I think maybe someone just borrowed your boat temporarily—because he needed it for the moment. You'll get it back. In the meantime, of course, you'll have to tell the owner it's been temporarily mislaid."

Barry shivered at the thought, and Alicia said, "That's not all. We're going to have to tell Aunt Ann and Uncle George where we've been. We're not supposed to be here, you see. But we did want to come and look——"

"I was coming to that," Mr. Kenyon said. He was leading the way along the path, taking long steps so that the girls almost had to run to keep up with him. "What did you come to look for? Or at?"

"We wanted to see the house," Barry said quickly.

"Why?"

"Well——" Barry looked at Alicia hopelessly. What could they say?

"Because there's some kind of mystery about it," Alicia said. "We don't know what it is, but we think that there's some go— oopf!" she finished as Barry deliberately backed into her cousin.

"Some what?" he asked. They couldn't see his face, but he sounded, Barry thought crossly, as though he could be laughing at them. Alicia had spoiled it anyway; she'd said enough to give the secret away probably, at least if he knew anything about it— and he must.

"Oh, we read about some old gold that was hidden away here," Barry said sheepishly. "Silly, I guess. But of course we wanted to come and look."

"Of course you did." He turned and smiled down at them. "Everybody wants to go looking for smuggled gold. That's perfectly natural."

I didn't say it was smuggled, Barry thought, so he *does* know the story.

"Let's go back a bit," Mr. Kenyon said casually. "Why did you think your borrowed boat would be in that little lake you told me about? Why not just rowed down the river? Or up it?"

"Because," Alicia said with a faintly triumphant air, "probably whoever took it is also looking for the gold."

Barry gasped. Maybe Alicia was right, but she hadn't thought that far herself, and she was surprised that Alicia had.

"Quite possibly," Mr. Kenyon agreed. "But why that lake?"

"Because we believe it runs into the river," Alicia went on. How she chatters! Barry thought grumpily. "And if somebody was being chased and dropped the gold, it'd be in that lake, wouldn't it? And you'd have to have a boat to hunt for it; if you had a boat, you could poke around with an oar or something."

Mr. Kenyon looked at her gravely. "Perhaps you're right. Yes, I see what you mean."

He walked on silently. Just then Barry caught a glimpse of the big tree lying on its side beyond the fence. "There's——" she began, but Mr. Kenyon walked on along the path. She followed him quietly. Maybe he knew a better place to climb over—not that she would ever take advantage of it some other day. Like Alicia, she wanted never to come back!

In a few minutes, they were at the big gate. Mr. Kenyon stopped, fished a key from his pocket, pulled the padlock toward him, and quickly unlocked it. Then he swung the gate open.

"There you are, kids," he said genially. "You go ahead. I think I'll take another look around for your boat."

"If you find it, let us know," Alicia began. "Then we——"

"I'm afraid you'd better go tell the owner that you've temporarily misplaced it," he said gently. "Even if I do find it this afternoon, I may not be able to get it back to you right away. I'm sorry, but you did lose it, you know, and you'll have to suffer a little bit. I'm sure we'll find it, though, and you can tell the owner that. Who does it belong to, by the way? I'll return it for you, if you like."

Barry explained, thanked him for his help, and humbly the two girls walked away. There were a couple of bad hours ahead of them, Barry knew, telling first Lester Graham about his boat, and then her parents. They'd have to confess about their escapade, she could see that now, and she knew she'd rather do it herself than have Mr. Kenyon or someone do it for her. Deep in imagined explanations, she was startled by Alicia's sudden question.

"Barry!" she gasped. "You know something awfully funny? How in the world did Mr. Kenyon happen to have a key to the gate?"

Chapter 10

The Story

Lester Graham's pudgy cheeks turned even more pale when Barry finished speaking.

"I told you I should go with you," he said angrily. "I never should have let you have the boat in the first place. My father will kill me. Where did you take it anyway, that someone stole it from you?"

Barry and Alicia had expected this question, and they had decided on a reply.

"Down beyond the new bridge," Barry reported. This was true, of course, as far as it went.

"Maybe some of the men working on the road swiped it," he suggested. "My father will go down and talk to the foreman."

"They aren't working today," Barry told him quickly. "There wasn't a soul around, Lester. Honest."

"Well, there *was*." Lester glared at Barry with his little piglike eyes. "Someone was there. Your father will have to pay for it, you know."

"But I've already told you—you're going to get it back."

"Yeah? Who'll bring it?"

"Mr. Kenyon. He's staying over at the Goulds'. He said he'd find it and bring it back to you himself."

"He did? Maybe he took it then." The same thing had occurred to the girls, but they had immediately dismissed the idea.

"Of course he didn't. He was—just there, out for a walk or something, and he said he'd find it for us."

"How could he be so sure?"

Barry sighed. Lester could ask more questions, she thought, and they were all good ones. "I don't know. But I believe him, and you should too."

"Why?" Lester kicked at a pebble.

"Well, if he doesn't, my father will pay for your old boat," Barry said hotly. "Don't you worry about that. Come on, Alicia."

"Bet you haven't told your father what you did," Lester called after them.

"I'm going to tell him right now." Barry tossed the words over her shoulder. "Oh, Alicia, I'd rather die than do it."

"I don't blame you," Alicia said sympathetically. "I'll keep my fingers crossed for you."

"You'd better keep them crossed for *us*," Barry told her. "And don't think you're not coming with me, because you are."

"But your father scares me."

"He scares me too, at times like this!" Barry assured her. "There he is on the porch. Come on, let's get it over with."

"Shouldn't we wash up first?"

"I don't want to do anything else first. I want to get it over with." Barry marched up the steps to the porch. Mr. Loomis, who was reading a newspaper, looked up and smiled.

"Hi, kids. Did you—oh, oh, I know that expression. What have you been up to?"

Barry took a deep breath, threw one last agonized look at

Alicia, and told the story she had been saying over and over to herself most of the way home. Mr. Loomis listened intently, his eyes moving occasionally from his daughter's face to his niece's, but he said nothing and his expression didn't change.

"And we're sorry," Barry finished at last. "Honest, Daddy."

"Sit down." Barry noticed with relief that his voice didn't sound angry. He spoke calmly and quietly. "Now, the fact that you came straight to me and told me the whole story shows that you know you've done wrong. That's clear enough, and in your favor. And you've had a good scare, I can see, so perhaps you realize just how foolish you've been. Before we decide anything, I have a couple of questions. First of all, why do you trust Paul Kenyon so much? The minute he told you he'd find the boat for you and return it, you believed him. Why?"

"He's so handsome, Uncle George," Alicia explained. "And he's terribly, terribly nice. He *couldn't* steal a boat. We're sure he's a government agent, or something exciting like that."

Mr. Loomis smiled. "They like to say that the bad men wear black hats and the good men wear white hats, so you can tell which is which. But it doesn't work out that way. And I'm sure being handsome doesn't have a thing to do with it."

"Besides, he had a key to the gate," Barry added earnestly. "Where would he get it? But if he wasn't supposed to have it, he wouldn't have opened the gate for us, would he?"

"He would if he wanted to get rid of you in a hurry! However, I know something about Paul Kenyon, and I'm sure he's all right. And not because he's handsome either. Don't think that every time you see someone who's good-looking you can decide he's one of the men with the white hats. All right, now for the other questions. What were you doing there anyway? I know you've always been fascinated by the place, Barry, but why all of a sudden, after all these years, do you decide to break the rules and go there?"

Barry threw Alicia a desperate look. They had expected this question too, and they had decided to evade a direct answer somehow, but Barry suspected it wasn't going to be possible.

"It's because of me, Uncle George," Alicia said. "I mean, Barry always wanted to go there and see the house, and now I did too, and because there were two of us just made it worse. Do you see?"

Mr. Loomis laughed. "I guess so," he admitted. "Yes, I think I can understand what you're trying to say. I also think that isn't all of it. There's too much going on in this town these days—too many strangers around, stirring up trouble and unrest. I guess it's only natural for you kids to catch the fever. And perhaps your mother and I have been wrong, Barry, in trying to keep you in the dark about the whole thing. That was a decision made long ago by all the adults in town, and we really hadn't much choice. But now that they've started to make the town over——"

He folded the newspaper neatly and put it on the table beside him.

"Yes," he said thoughtfully, "I guess it's time you heard the whole story. But I haven't forgotten that there's some unfinished business here. We'll get back to that later, and decide on just what punishment you've earned for yourselves. First, I'll fill you in on the background of whatever it is you've heard."

Alicia, who was sitting on a square leather hassock, hugged her knees with excitement, and Barry, on the floor, leaned back against the wall, curling her fingers into her palms.

"More than a hundred years ago," Mr. Loomis began, "before the Civil War, people started what was called the Underground Railroad. This was a method of getting Negro slaves who wanted to escape from their owners up north and into Canada, where they could hide and not be forced to come back. There were many routes, of course, and the poor slaves hurried from one place to another in the dead of night, hiding by day. They were sheltered and fed by families who lived along the way. A good many of the Negroes got to Northville, and the last stop for them before Canada was the Parrish house, which had just been built by the first Parrish to live in this town.

"That place was picked because it was on the river, and as you know, Barry, North River flows into the St. Lawrence in Canada, a good many miles from here. The fugitives were harbored in the Parrish cellars or outbuildings for a few days, then put into boats at night, and drifted or rowed downstream and across to the Canadian border. I don't know how many tired and frightened people went through Northville at that time, but I guess it was a sizable number."

Barry was watching her father with a puzzled frown. She had learned about the Underground Railroad in school, but she had never heard that Northville had anything to do with it.

"Well," Mr. Loomis went on, "as history tells us, eventually the Underground Railroad was no longer used or necessary. People forgot all about it, and the part the Parrishes had played in the whole thing was forgotten, too. But in the 1930's, this country went off the gold standard. It became illegal to possess gold, it was impossible to get gold coins, and people like jewelers who needed gold for their work were forced to buy under strict quotas from certain approved sources. At the same time, Canada was finding and opening up new gold mines. I guess you can see what happened. There were unscrupulous manufacturers who wanted gold so badly that they would pay high prices for quantities of it. And there were unscrupulous men who would undertake to smuggle the gold out of Canada and into the States, to get that money.

"Sooner or later, it was inevitable that someone would remember the way across the border in the northern direction and take it into his head to use the same route in reverse. Gold was rowed or paddled or perhaps sent upstream in a small motorboat, sneaked across the border in the middle of the night, and eventually found its way to the Parrish land. I don't know how long they got away with it. Naturally, the police of both countries were doing everything they could to stop this illegal trade. The story is that one night the smugglers thought they were about to be caught, so they buried a big supply of it. By this time most of the culprits had been caught, and the gold they were carrying at the time had been recovered. This is generally thought to have been the very last attempt to smuggle the gold through Northville, and the rumor that the loot was dumped here still persists."

Alicia squirmed with delight. "Oh, this is exciting," she breathed.

"But if that gold was found," Barry asked, "wouldn't it have to go back where it came from? Or is there a reward?"

"If someone does find it—if, in fact, there's anything to be found, because the whole thing may be just a tall tale—it's a case of finders keepers, I understand. The mine from which it was presumably stolen long ago closed down, and let it be known that they wouldn't search for it, nor would they demand its return if found."

"Would there be a whole lot?" Alicia asked.

"From the point of view of a productive mine, probably not. But if you and Barry should discover it, you'd have enough for your college educations with some left over for those convertibles you're always talking about," he said with a twinkle in his eyes.

Barry's head swam with visions of chests full of gold coins. "But why has it been such a big fat secret?" she asked, pouting. "Look at all the time we've wasted, Daddy!"

Mr. Loomis laughed. "There are a good many reasons," he told her gently. "First of all, all sorts of people have been attracted to the town, looking for it. The worst kind of people, usually. Some years ago there was a tragedy because of that gold. Philip Parrish, the last of the same family to live in the house, got killed because of it. Or at least, everyone always thought so. He heard noises or saw lights or something that made him suspicious one night, and he went out to investigate. Anyway, that's what is thought to have happened. He had mentioned being worried about trespassers before. When his wife woke up in the morning, he wasn't in the house. Later that day they found him dead. He had been fatally attacked, and on that same day a man who had lived for years in the town disappeared."

"Uncle Louis!" cried Alicia.

Mr. Loomis looked at her in surprise. Then he nodded. "Yes, Uncle Louis. He was sort of an odd character whom no one knew very well, but he had worked for the Parrishes for years. No one could believe that he would harm Philip Parrish, but we didn't understand why he disappeared, either. It was suggested that he had, willingly or unwillingly, gone away with whoever it was who'd been prowling. Some people even remembered that he had said once that he had himself done some smuggling.

"Anyway," he went on, "the consensus was that Uncle Louis and the gold had somehow gone together, and it was a great relief to most of us here in town, because we thought it would put an end to the treasure-hunters. It was hardly a relief to the family, though, with Philip dead, and his friends said he himself had counted on finding the gold to put the family back on its feet financially."

"What happened to them? His wife, I mean," Alicia asked.

"She closed up the house, and she and her baby went to live with her folks somewhere, I think. She had the fence built to protect the property, since she'd been warned that the public might run loose over it because of the gold rumor. I think she used all of the money that was in a trust fund of her husband's to pay taxes and all that, because she couldn't bring herself to sell the place."

Barry sighed. It seemed to her that the story had no happy ending. The gold was gone, and that was that.

"We all got together," Mr. Loomis said, "and decided that the gold had been removed and we wanted it forgotten by everyone. We were especially determined that the youngsters growing up in this town should never hear about it. We did a good job too, didn't we?" he added boyishly. "Frankly, I was one of those who said it couldn't be done."

"But—what happened?" Alicia demanded.

"The roads happened, that's what. And some idiot wrote a syndicated story that ran in half the newspapers in the country reviving that old buried-treasure business."

"Do you think the gold *is* still there, Uncle George?" asked Alicia, her brown eyes shining. "All that money! Gold coins, imagine!"

"*I* don't know, Alicia. Haven't you been listening to me? No one knows, of course. And it wouldn't be in the form of coins, but of ingots, bars of pure gold. People call them goldbricks. And whether or not there *are* any of them around, I don't intend to have you youngsters searching. Have I made that clear?"

"Yes, Uncle George," Alicia said quickly, and Barry nodded glumly.

"Good. And now, what will we do about this little escapade of yours? Let me see, supposing we decide that——"

"I think, Your Honor, that leniency should be in order, due to extenuating circumstances."

They all looked toward the door. Mr. Kenyon stood there, a long thin shape dimly seen through the screen.

"Mr. Kenyon, come in!" Barry's father called heartily.

"You asked me to drop by one day, and here I am," Paul Kenyon said. He walked across the porch with a nod at Barry and Alicia, and sat down on the wicker couch. Just then Barry's mother came out from the house and Mr. Loomis introduced their guest to her.

"But I didn't come only because of that invitation," Mr. Kenyon said, when everyone had settled down. "I really came to see your girls. First of all, the boat is back with its owner. And all is forgiven—in that quarter anyway."

"Boat? What boat?" Mrs. Loomis asked.

"We'll go into that later, Ann," her husband told her. "Barry and Alicia, thank Mr. Kenyon."

"We do, we do!" Barry cried. "Thank you, Mr. Kenyon."

"And since I interrupted your discussion of punishment," Mr. Kenyon went on smoothly, "may I say something? I never interfere in a family's affairs, and I know that no one should try to butt into such a matter, but just this once I'm going to break my own rule. You see, Mr. Loomis, the girls know they did wrong, and they've suffered probably more than you realize. It's pretty scary in those woods, and having their boat spirited away from them, depriving them of their only means of getting out, and then having a stranger appear out of the shadows—well, it seems to me that fate got ahead of you when it came to handing out punishment."

Mr. Loomis sighed and shrugged his shoulders. Mrs. Loomis looked completely baffled. Alicia and Barry crossed their fingers and waited.

"Also, I'd like to say that the temptation was unusually great. After all, not every town has a lot of gold hidden inside its limits somewhere. Maybe this one doesn't either, but there are so many people around who think that it does, it's understandable for every girl and boy within a ten-mile radius to catch the fever. In my opinion, these two have paid for their mistakes. Now, I've spoken my piece and I won't say any more." He turned to the girls and gave them his slow smile. "I've done what I could, kids," he added.

"Barry, just so long as you don't think you're ever going to get off scot-free again in your whole life," Mr. Loomis said, after a moment's thought. "And you too, Alicia. I believe you'll never forget this experience, so I'll let you off just this once. Just this once, remember."

The girls nodded solemnly. The whole scene seemed unreal to Barry—having Mr. Kenyon on their own porch, his pleading for them with her father, and her father taking it so calmly and agreeing to forget about punishing them. He was right in thinking they'd never forget it, or expect to be so lucky another time.

"And there's someone else here who has, unwittingly, provided a little punishment of his own," Mr. Kenyon added. "May I ask him to come in?" The Loomises nodded, and he called out to the car, "Come on in, Charlie, please." Barry, peering through the screen door, could just see a round figure climbing out of Mr. Kenyon's car. It was the fat man who was staying at the Goulds, and he was surprisingly spry and agile for a man so stockily built.

"This is Mr. Vachon, and he has something to say," Mr. Kenyon remarked. "It has a bearing on all of this, as you will see."

Mr. Vachon looked around solemnly, sat down on the edge of a chair, and began, "I am sorry, little girl." He was, to Barry's astonishment, speaking directly to Alicia. "I am sorry to scare you."

"M-me?" stammered Alicia.

"Yes. You were on that path near the fence and alone, and I think no little girl should be there that way. So I scare you. I make the noise like dog——" He panted vigorously, his tongue lolling ridiculously from his mouth. "And with the feet." Now he stamped on the wooden floor of the porch. "But only to make you run away from that place. You did, yes?" He chuckled cheerfully.

Alicia nodded, and Barry caught a quizzical look thrown by her father toward his niece. Oh, golly, *more* explanations, she thought.

"You should not go there like that," Mr. Vachon told Alicia gently, shaking his head from side to side reprovingly. "Who knows who is there also?"

"Tell them why you were there," Mr. Kenyon suggested.

"Uncle Louis—Louis LeBlanc—was my friend. He knew the place well; he go there much. To look for the gold which was smuggled there."

"Charlie, tell the rest. It has been said around the town that Louis himself smuggled gold. You say it isn't true."

"Oh, no!" Mr. Vachon looked shocked. "Louis would not smuggle gold. Never, never."

"But he told someone that he was guilty of smuggling. Can you tell us what it was he smuggled?" Mr. Kenyon's blue eyes were sharp and bright, fastened on Mr. Vachon's round, pink face.

Mr. Vachon turned less pink. He hung his head and stared nervously at the painted floor of the porch.

"Well, did he ever engage in any smuggling?" prodded Mr. Kenyon.

"Just once—just once he smuggle something," Mr. Vachon said in a low voice. "Just the once, Mr. Kenyon."

"And what was it?" Mr. Kenyon asked firmly.

"Me," said Mr. Vachon simply. He raised his eyes and looked humbly at Mr. Kenyon. "Just that once, he smuggle. He smuggle me."

Chapter 11

Chris Again

The round little man's story had not interested the girls too much, but they listened politely. Smuggling Charlie Vachon was far less exciting than smuggling gold. Besides, it had been so simple. Mr. Vachon explained that Uncle Louis crossed the border so often, when he visited his French-Canadian friends living nearby, that he was well known at the border. He often brought his friends across for a few hours, or a day or two, but when he had driven Mr. Vachon back with him, it had not been for a visit but for good.

"At the time," Mr. Vachon had explained, "I was young and wanted to get to the great United States. I think it the end to poverty and trouble, you see. Soon I find that poverty depends on me and what I do with my hands and my brains, not on where I live. One day I go back home, and later I come here again—only legal this time. And now," he had added proudly, "I am U.S.

citizen. But poor Louis; by then he is dead, so he does not know. I think it always trouble him—what he did about me."

The story did have the advantage, Barry thought, of taking everyone's mind off her and Alicia. Later, when she pointed this out to her cousin, she added, "I was holding my breath for fear Daddy would change his mind. But he got so wrapped up in Mr. Vachon and everything that he forgot us, and now it's too late for him to decide to punish us after all, don't you think?"

"My father always says the real reason for punishment is so you'll remember you did wrong and won't do it again," Alicia replied. "Uncle George said we'd never forget what we did—and he's right!"

"We were lucky Mr. Kenyon came along when he did. I'm sure Daddy wouldn't have let us off so easy if he hadn't."

Except for a little discussion of Mr. Vachon's story, nothing more had been said about the boat or the rest of the cousins' escapade. Mr. Loomis had reported that Bernie Jones had someone patrolling the fence full time, and when Barry said she thought that had been true all along, he had admitted that Bernie Jones had merely given out the news in the hope it would frighten people off the property. But now he really had deputies keeping watch over it in earnest.

"Well," said Alicia, one afternoon after they'd been home from school for a little while, "now no one could object if we went to the Parrish house—outside the fence, I mean. Wouldn't you like to see that pool again, Barry? There'd be nothing to be scared of, because if we yelled one of the deputies would come running."

Barry had been thinking along the same lines, and they set out at once. It was nice to know they wouldn't be scared any more but, she reflected, it did take some of the fun out of it.

"Good thing we're wearing jeans," Barry remarked as they

passed, for the first time, the fallen tree trunk, left the path, and approached the location of the pool. "If this was still summer and we had shorts on, our legs would be a mess."

Alicia looked around nervously. "Now that we're here, it's just as bad as ever," she complained. "Where's that man who's patroling?"

"He'll be along. There's the pool!" Barry stared at the dark water. "It's like a road, Alicia, and it looks as though someone had dug it. And see that big, flat rock? I bet that's where they pulled the boats up and loaded the people on."

"What people?"

"The slaves on the Underground Railroad, silly."

"Um." Alicia looked around vaguely. "Come on, Barry; we've seen it. Let's go home."

They began to push their way back to the path. Barry had taken only a few steps, after one last look at the dark water, when Alicia whispered, "Shh. Listen."

Barry heard it too, and some of her old fear returned. Then she remembered. "It's one of Bernie Jones's men," she said in a low voice. "Why do we always get so petrified here?"

The color came back to their faces and they smiled sheepishly. But when Alicia, who had been peering ahead, spoke again she whispered out of habit.

"I see a blue shirt," she announced. "Maybe it's Roy Upton. I don't want to meet him here, do you?"

"I hear a voice. A woman's voice, I think. Do you suppose it's that waitress who was near here before?"

The voices grew louder. Barry found herself looking around for a place to hide, but she reminded herself sternly that that was no longer necessary. They had as much right on this path as anyone, and there was a deputy within call if they needed him.

At that moment, a figure rounded the bend in the path.

"Chris!" cried Barry and Alicia together. It was Chris Clark, and he was with the waitress from Milly's.

"I didn't know you had a blue shirt!" Alicia exclaimed resentfully.

After one startled look at her, Chris threw back his head and laughed. "Is there a law against it? What are you two doing here?"

"What are you?" countered Barry. "All those times you said you wouldn't come when we asked you to. And now——"

She stopped, realizing that she had been talking as though the woman didn't exist. Covered with confusion, she stood there, wondering what to say next.

It was the woman herself who spoke. She smiled at the girls and said, "Chris, I think perhaps we should explain to your friends."

Chris's face darkened, and he shook his head.

"Yes, Chris, really."

"Well, all right." He looked at the woman for a moment, then turned to face the cousins. "This is my mother," he said curtly.

Barry managed, she hoped, not to show her complete amazement. She murmured "How do you do" politely and looked from one to the other. They did look alike—now that she knew their relationship. The same light hair, blue eyes, and long, thin faces.

"I know who you are," the woman said, smiling. "Chris has told me all about you. And of course you've been in Milly's. Tell me, Alicia, why are you so surprised to see Chris wearing a blue shirt? I brought a couple with me when I came, but there's nothing odd about them, is there?"

"We never saw him wear one before," Alicia explained. "Always a white shirt. We thought he was somebody else, because of the blue shirt."

"Who?" Chris demanded.

"Roy Upton," Alicia confessed, and Chris scowled. "But, Chris, have you been sleeping in the boathouse?" she asked.

"Why should you think that?" Chris's mother asked quickly.

"Because there's a blue shirt hanging on a nail there. And there's also a cot with a blanket, Mrs. Clark," Alicia explained quickly.

"How do you know about that?" Chris asked angrily. "No, I haven't been sleeping there, although I know someone has. But how did you get there? You're not supposed to go over the fence."

"Neither are you!" Barry reminded him.

"How *did* you get there?" The voice was low and gentle, but somehow it made Barry realize that Chris's mother expected an answer.

"We borrowed a boat and—and rowed there," Barry confessed.

"I bet your father didn't like that," Chris remarked with a grin.

"He didn't. Specially since someone stole the boat."

"Who? Where did they take it?"

"We don't know," Alicia told Chris. "Barry, we never even asked Mr. Kenyon."

"Whose boat? Did you tell the police? Where was it when it was taken?" Chris's questions spilled forth.

"Chris, not so many questions," his mother said, putting a warning hand on his arm.

"I know, but this could be important."

"It belonged to Lester Graham. And Mr. Kenyon found it for us, but he didn't tell us where. And now he's gone away, I think." Barry was sure she saw an expression of relief on Chris's face, and on his mother's also, but she couldn't understand why it should make any difference to them.

"What were you snooping around there for in the first place?" Chris flung at them suddenly. "What did you hope to find?"

"Gold!" cried Alicia. "I mean, there might be some gold buried there."

"Well, keep your noses out of it," Chris said crossly.

"Chris, I'm ashamed of you. I think your friends want to help."

"Help? Well, you see, Mrs. Clark——" Alicia began.

The woman interrupted her with an apologetic smile. "I'm not Mrs. Clark," she said gently. "Clark is the name Chris decided to use—it's his middle name. And I'm not Mrs. Conway, either. That's the name I gave Milly. I'm Ellen Parrish."

"Mother!" Chris said, in a belated effort to stop her.

"I think these girls should know," Mrs. Parrish said. "And I want them to hear why we're here, too. You see, when Northville got all this publicity, it was Chris's idea that if people were reminded of—of the gold and all that, they might come pouring into Northville and start looking around. He wanted to get here first. The Bassetts worked for Chris's grandfather, and they agreed to take him in if he'd pay for his room and board by working around the place. They're the only ones who know who he is, by the way, except for Paul Kenyon. He's very clever and he guessed right away. I gave him the key to the gate, and he's been helping us all he can."

She smiled at the girls and added, "I hadn't really planned to come here myself. I thought after a while Chris would get the whole business out of his system and leave, but finally I decided to come and see what was going on. I was terribly afraid someone would recognize me and stir up a lot of talk. It seemed important to us both that no one should know who we are. But apparently no one guessed. The local people don't eat in Milly's, so that was all right, and although Milly herself lived in town when I did, we never happened to meet then.

"Anyway, here we are. You won't tell anyone, will you? It'd be better to keep it a secret as long as we can. Chris is convinced the gold is still around somewhere and that we're going to find it. And you'll help us, won't you?"

"If we can!" Alicia breathed, her eyes shining.

"Of course we'll help," Barry agreed. "But Mrs. Clark—I mean, Mrs. Parrish—would you mind terribly if we just told my family? About you and Chris, I mean. You see——"

Mrs. Parrish smiled warmly at Barry. "You've already been in trouble with them, haven't you? Of course you may tell them, Barry. I wouldn't want it any other way. But no one else. Agreed?"

"Yes, oh *yes*," the cousins said fervently.

It had been hard for Barry to accept the fact that Chris and his mother were actually the owners of River House, which is what they themselves called the Parrish place. She had looked at it with longing for so long that it didn't seem right to have a perfect stranger like Chris walk up and claim it. Although that was silly, she scolded herself. It had belonged to Chris, or to his family anyway, all along, and she had known of course that somewhere in the world there were people who owned it. The girls had asked Barry's father if Chris and his mother would live in the house now that they were back, and Mr. Loomis had said he supposed that would "depend."

"Which," Alicia said darkly, "is what grownups always say when they want you to mind your own business!" And Barry agreed with her.

"There's one good thing," Barry remarked as they walked slowly along the road on their way home from Miller's. "That awful Roy Upton has gone."

"He was the horrors," Alicia agreed.

The gasoline station was operating now, but an older man was in charge. Because of its location, the new station seemed to attract more than its share of business, which the girls had resented while Roy was still there, but now that he'd dropped out of sight, it didn't seem so important.

At that moment, a car pulled up beside them on the road. "Hi, kids, get in," said Mr. Kenyon's voice. "I'll ride you right up your own driveway. I'm on my way to see your father, Barry. Is he home, do you think?"

Barry and Alicia pushed their grocery bags into the back of the car, and scrambled in beside Mr. Kenyon.

"I guess so," Barry answered. "He's building a patio, and it's slow work, he says."

"I'll bet it is." Mr. Kenyon drove up to the house with a flourish and reached across the girls to open the car door on their side. "Never mind the groceries; I'll carry them in."

When Mr. Loomis saw the visitor, he smiled happily. "Hurray for an interruption," he said. "I've had about enough of this. Unless you'd like to help?"

"Not me. Sit down and rest for a minute. I'm happy to provide you with an excuse." Mr. Loomis sat down on the low wall around the space he was paving with big, flat stones. Mrs. Loomis came out from the kitchen, perched beside him, and coaxed him into putting on his sweater. Mr. Kenyon and the girls sat on a garden bench that had been moved aside so that Mr. Loomis could work in the corner area.

"Now," said Mr. Kenyon dramatically, "I'll tell you why I'm here."

Chapter 12

Pot of Gold

"I am the bearer of an invitation," Mr. Kenyon announced, looking around and noting that he had the full attention of each of them. "Specifically an invitation to these young ladies, but you two are included—if you want to be included."

Barry and Alicia were all ears. They looked at each other excitedly. At last something was going to happen that they weren't to be cut off from.

"Ellen Parrish—I believe you know who I mean, although you may not have met her?" He turned to Mrs. Loomis, who nodded and murmured, "Of course." "Well," Mr. Kenyon went on, "Ellen and her son have asked me to suggest to these young detectives that they might like to be in on the doings tomorrow morning."

"Doings?" asked Mr. Loomis.

"The Parrishes and I are going to have a good look around— with a couple of other people who have some knowledge of the matter," Mr. Kenyon explained. "I've finally convinced Ellen that things should be cleared up once and for all. She has agreed to one big search party, which I've assured her will not necessarily encourage everyone within a fifty-mile radius to attempt the same thing. I thought the girls would like to be among those present. Wouldn't you?"

"Oh, *yes!*" Alicia and Barry squealed in duet.

"And you two, would you———"

"Wild horses couldn't keep us away," Mr. Loomis said solemnly. "And that goes for both of us, Paul."

" 'Paul'? Since when?" Barry and Alicia signaled the message to each other.

"All right then. The expedition sets forth at ten o'clock, rain or shine. No, maybe only if it's 'shine.' We'll make another date if it should rain. Suppose we all meet at the big gate—which will be wide open for once. See you then."

Barry and Alicia spent the next few hours staring at the sky. A constant fleet of white puffy clouds sailed across the blue sea overhead, threatening tomorrow's sunshine. When they went to bed that night, there wasn't a single star to be seen.

"Barry, I'll just *die* if it rains," Alicia said. "I couldn't bear waiting a whole day, could you?"

They were sure they wouldn't sleep a wink, but Barry opened her eyes to find Alicia standing at her bedside. "I just woke up," Alicia said, yawning. "Look! It's a bee-yoo-ti-ful day!"

Barry saw that it had rained in the night, and the red and yellow leaves remaining on the trees looked washed and polished. The sky had never seemed more blue. The girls dressed quickly in jeans and T-shirts. Even Barry's mother, who seldom wore pants, had on her old gardening dungarees, and she looked fully as excited as her daughter and niece.

"The big day!" she exclaimed. "I made pancakes. You'll need a lot of them, to keep up your strength."

At a quarter to ten they climbed into Mr. Loomis' car and drove away.

"Can't you go any faster, Daddy?" Barry moaned.

"And have Bernie Jones pinch me for speeding? We'll be there at ten o'clock. Don't worry about *that*," he answered.

It seemed odd to drive down the dusty road in a car, even odder to drive through the Parrish gate. Mr. Loomis pulled in beside Mr. Kenyon's car, and almost immediately Mr. Kenyon appeared and closed the gate.

"Don't want to give the idea we're holding open house," he remarked. "Well, you kids look ready for action. Follow me."

Barry looked around with interest. The shadows weren't so deep and thick today. The house, although not exactly cheerful-looking, appeared to be merely a big wooden building with nothing spooky about it. The tangle of the thicket wasn't ominous. The bushes and trees and grass looked uncared for, but not threatening. It was not only because of the bright morning sun, she knew. It was because she was here openly, not secretly, and because there were so many people around. Besides Mr. Kenyon and the four Loomises, there were Chris and his mother, Mr. and Mrs. Bassett, Mr. Vachon, and Mr. and Mrs. Marble.

"This is quite a search party," Mr. Kenyon said cheerfully. "Everyone here has at least one idea about where the goldbricks might be. Probably one of you is right. So go to it! The front and back doors of the house are unlocked and open, and Ellen Parrish says we may go in and out as we choose. The two small side gates are open too, so anyone who wants to investigate the other side of the fence may do so. We have only one regulation today: no one is to go anywhere away from the rest of us alone. Is that understood? Always with someone. In other words, the buddy system."

Barry was thrilled at his words until Alicia muttered in her ear, "That regulation is just for us kids, what do you bet?" Barry knew her cousin was undoubtedly right. Still, the fact that they were here at all was good enough for her.

Everyone stood stock still for a moment, as though waiting for Mr. Kenyon to blow a whistle to release them, Barry thought. She soon discovered they were also waiting for information.

"We're looking," he said, glancing around the circle of faces, "for some or all of a small load of goldbricks that was presumably hidden here years ago. Hidden or buried, perhaps. There may not be any at all, as we know, but for Ellen's sake, and Chris's, I hope there are. Because, and I'm sure everyone here agrees on this, if we do find some, they'll belong to the Parrishes, and would probably enable them to live in the Parrish house again— and that's as it should be."

Barry's eyes met Chris's. She forgot she had resented his owning the house. Instead she saw the desperate look on his face, the mute appeal in his eyes, and she thought what fun it would be to have for a friend the boy who lived in that big, beautiful house. Because, painted and lived in, it would be beautiful, she knew.

"Before we start our search," Mr. Kenyon went on, "I'd better tell you that unless you have some inside information that provides you with a special reason for doing it, I'd skip the dock. It's been thoroughly covered. Incidentally, you girls discovered that someone was living in the old boathouse. As you may have guessed by now, it was Roy Upton, who was doing a little treasure-hunting on his own. He fixed himself up there so he could stay overnight and do his digging and hunting in the early morning, when no one would see him. But he got careless and began to leave his things here, so Bernie Jones sort of recommended that if he left town, he wouldn't be arrested for trespassing. He took your boat, too, by the way; I was sure he had. We're well rid of that young man. Anyway, as I was saying, the dock is in bad shape, and if anyone wants to go out there, I suggest he let me know first, so we can keep an eye on him." He looked around. "On your mark. Get set. And—go!" he said.

The others broke away from the circle, but Barry and Alicia stood there uncertainly. After one last look around, Mr. Kenyon walked over to them and said, "You two are here because you had one of the best theories I've heard. Better hop to it, before someone else stakes out a claim on your private pool or inlet or whatever it is. See, I opened that little gate so you can get out."

Barry suddenly understood. She looked around, getting her bearings. "I never saw that door in the fence. Come on, Alicia."

"There it is!" Alicia shouted after a few minutes. "Ouch, be careful. The branches on these bushes are so sharp."

Barry followed Alicia to the edge of the water. A splashing noise made them jump, and they turned quickly toward the sound. Almost immediately they saw Chris, wading up from the river toward where they were standing. He was wearing rubber boots that reached to his hips.

"Hi," he said. "I thought you'd be here. I'm sure your theory is right. Mr. K. does too, but he said he'd let us kids work it out on our own." He grinned, his blue eyes bright with excitement. "And that's what we're going to do."

"Chris," Barry said crossly, "what do you mean, our 'theory'? Mr. Kenyon said the same thing. We don't know what you're talking about."

"You're not as smart as I thought you were then." Chris pretended to grumble. "Of course you remember. You told him you thought someone took the boat so he could use it to try to find the gold."

"Yes, but——"

"And you said that this water was part of the river and it used to come up higher."

"Anybody would know that," Barry objected.

"Sure. Mr. Kenyon knew it. He even knew that this ravine

was a man-made canal, sort of, that went up close to the house. This was where they brought up the boats so the slaves could get in at night and get rowed to the river and down across the border. He knew all that."

"Then what's all this business about our theory?" Barry demanded. She looked at him suspiciously to make sure he wasn't laughing at her.

"You—one of you—said something about the river not being so high now. Of course he knew that too——"

"Oh, Chris, are you trying to confuse us?" Alicia wailed. "If we didn't tell him anything he didn't know, what's the point of all this?"

"Then," Chris went on, pointedly ignoring the interruption, "you said something about dropping the gold overboard when they were being chased."

"And Mr. Kenyon also knew that," Barry said drily. "No doubt."

"That's where you're wrong," Chris announced happily. "Everyone always took it for granted that the gold was hidden here deliberately, and that for some reason or other nobody came back for it. They made a lot of arrests all at once, you know, and the smuggling stopped. But you gave him the idea that the gold might have simply been scuttled, which would make a difference about where to look. Goldbricks are heavy and hard to carry, so if someone was being chased he'd toss them overboard, Mr. Kenyon says. So——"

"Who *is* Mr. Kenyon?" Alicia demanded. "And how come he knows so much?"

"He's——" Chris looked around suddenly. "Look, we're wasting time with all this jawing. I'll tell you later. We're here to find the gold, remember? I like it in Northville, and I want to stay here. I'd like to live in my father's house, too. But we've got to have some money to do that, and besides, we don't want everyone in the world running all over our land, looking for buried treasure. If we find it, that'll stop. Don't you see? Now, let's *look*. I've got on boots, so I'll start digging around with this old hoe and see if I hit anything under the water. And you two—here, one of you use this shovel. It's small, but it's pretty heavy, so you'll have to take turns or you'll knock yourselves out. And here's a big stick, for the other one."

Alicia seized the shovel from his hands and began to dig wildly. Barry smiled at her cousin's fierce expression, and turned to watch Chris slash away beneath the surface of the water with his hoe. Then she stood still, listening to voices calling back and forth in the distance. By the sounds, she could tell that her father was at the river's edge with Mr. Vachon, and she saw her mother hurry into the house with Mrs. Parrish. Barry suspected that her mother wasn't terribly interested in the treasure hunt, but she'd always longed to see the inside of the Parrish house. The Bassetts were slowly making their way around the house, apparently searching through the ruined flowerbeds, and Barry could just glimpse the Marbles on the far side of the property, working along the fence there.

Everyone working, she thought. Everyone—but me! And she began prodding away along the edges of the inlet with the big stick Chris had given her. "This is crazy," she said aloud, after half an hour of futile probing and prodding. "Mr. Kenyon has been over this whole place a jillion times, I bet." She looked around to see him standing not far away, regarding her thoughtfully. Now how long has he been there? she wondered. He tossed her a smile and turned away. "He just sort of hopes we'll fall over something," she added shrewdly, carrying on her muttered monologue, "but he doesn't expect anything, not *really*."

She looked around again cautiously, to make sure that Paul Kenyon wasn't still watching her, then she stopped making even a pretense of working. Alicia too had stopped; she had tossed her shovel in Barry's direction and was sitting with her back against a young tree, nursing her sore palms.

Chris, who had been splashing noisily around all this time, saw Barry standing idle and waded over to her.

"I get the feeling we're wasting our time," he said with a tired smile.

"So do I." Barry kicked at the handle of the shovel lying at her feet. "Chris, do they *know* those goldbricks were brought in a boat?"

"They caught a lot of people doing the smuggling with boats. Besides, it's the only thing that makes sense. Anyhow, why do you ask?"

"No reason." Barry sighed.

"That was why it all happened here," Chris explained scowling. "The Underground Railroad, the river, the border so close—all that."

"I know," Barry nodded. She didn't blame Chris for being reluctant to give up the idea of the gold, but she was rapidly losing faith in it herself. "Oh, dear. When I lose something, like my notebook—and I'm always losing that—my father always says, 'Where would you go if you were a notebook?' And I usually find it." She giggled. "Where would you go if you were a goldbrick?"

Chris smiled at her. "To a goldbrickyard, of course," he said. "So all we——"

"But, Chris—that's it! The brickyard!" Barry stood up straight and stared at him.

"The brickyard? But that hasn't been used for years. It's——" He pulled off his rubber boots quickly. "Come on," he urged her, his blue eyes blazing with excitement.

Barry ran after him, then stopped. "We've got to get Alicia," she said.

"Why? You thought of it. Come *on*. And be quiet, so no one will know what we're up to."

"Alicia has been in this all along," Barry insisted stubbornly. "It wouldn't be fair to leave her out of it now."

"OK, get her. But hurry."

Barry ran back and said in a low voice, "Alicia, we've thought of something. Come on, but be quiet. We don't want the others to notice where we're going."

Alicia gave her one startled and inquiring look and scrambled to her feet. The three moved quickly to the path, and then hurried across the clearing at the back of the house. As soon as he considered they were out of sight and earshot of the grownups, Chris broke into a run.

"Where are we going?" Alicia asked.

"Here." Chris turned along the fence, which ran through the deserted brickyard. The collapsed shed with its broken loading platform was outside; the ruined kiln, fallen chimney, and a small pile of dirty weathered bricks were inside.

"Here? But why?"

"It was Barry's idea," Chris said. "She said where would a brick go—never mind that now. Come on; let's break them up."

"How?" Barry picked up a dust-covered brick and stared at it.

"Like this." He threw a brick with all his might against a boulder behind the clearing. It fell to the ground unbroken. "Heck. Well, keep trying. Hurry up. If the goldbricks were hidden here, they'd have to be inside, don't you see? Made to look like regular bricks. Get busy!"

Barry was fast losing her enthusiasm. She felt even more silly throwing bricks at a rock than she had pushing a stick into shallow water, but she did as she was told. The third brick she reached for surprised her.

"Hey, this one is heavy," she said. "It——"

Chris grabbed it from her and tossed it, with both hands, at the boulder. It made a solid *thunk* as it hit, and split apart.

"That's it!" Chris all but screamed in his excitement. "See, the gold bar is there inside. They just put a kind of a thick shell of clay around it, and baked it to make it look like a regular brick."

Barry and Alicia ran to look. It was disappointing, Barry thought. Wrapped in dirty cloth was a small object about the size of a candy bar. "Is this all it is?"

"All! Quick, let's see how many there are. Pick out the heavy bricks." Chris was scrabbling away through the remaining bricks in the untidy heap, occasionally throwing one aside with a crow of satisfaction.

"So, the young heads were wiser after all."

They turned to see Mr. Kenyon grinning widely at them. Near him, the round face of Mr. Vachon peered anxiously. The others were close behind.

"They have found it, the gold? Here? But of course, of course!" Mr. Vachon exclaimed. "Louis, he say to me the loading place, or something like that. I think he means the dock, the way I told you, Mr. Kenyon. Then, after you tell me what the young lady say about throwing from the boat, I think he meant the landing place where they have the running-away people get into boat in the old days. But he mean this one. And I see, too, how it happen. Louis, he always has bricks rattling around in his old truck. He says he likes the sound, and also he enjoys saying to his friends, 'Help yourself, take what you like.' He is so friendly that he wants to give to people always. He likes to have them say, 'Louis, I need ten, maybe eleven bricks to fix wall,' and Louis says, 'Help yourself. I got plenty.' "

Mr. Vachon's face was sad as he watched Chris and Mr. Kenyon carefully sort the heavy bricks from the others. "But these friends," he went on, "they are not good. They take advantage of Louis and his big heart. They put other bricks in with his, up there in Canada, and then one of them rides down with him to visit. When Louis is not looking, is when they take their own

special bricks away. I see now. Louis does not know—I stake my life on that. He would not smuggle gold, Louis. You must believe this."

"We believe you, Charlie," Mr. Kenyon assured him. "And of course that must be exactly what happened."

"I think now," Mr. Vachon went on earnestly, "that Louis had some way found out about these bricks. He go to see Mr. Parrish even though it is middle of the night—he is so excited. And he find Mr. Parrish there in woods, near brickyard, and he is dead. Poor Louis, he is frightened that people will say it is his fault. Now I see Mr. Parrish must have been killed by the man who had just come down across the border with Louis, and who brought this gold. He—that man—must have run away, and been afraid to come back to get it.

"I should have made poor Louis tell me plain, before he died," Mr. Vachon went on mournfully. "I did not listen good. When I see story in the paper about Louis' niece, Michele Marble, and the motel, and the gold, I remember a little. But mostly I come here to see Michele, and to tell her—and Mrs. Parrish—that Louis did not do anything bad to Mr. Parrish."

"We've always known that," Mrs. Parrish said quickly. They were all there now, watching excitedly. "Philip and Uncle Louis were fond of each other. He shouldn't have been afraid," she added.

"There's something I don't understand," Mr. Loomis said slowly. "Uncle Louis made bricks himself—he would know about bricks. These look different, even to me. If they hadn't been covered with dust, all of them, you could see at a glance something was wrong. Why wouldn't Uncle Louis realize he'd got some strange bricks mixed up with his?"

"These terrible men," Mr. Vachon explained, "they would be too smart to let Louis see their bricks. They could manage to take from truck and put in pile with the others, then soon take away. Louis never know about it, I would swear to that."

"Then why were they all mixed up?" Barry asked. "Wouldn't the men put their funny bricks together in a pile?"

"That may have happened when the fence was built," Mr. Kenyon suggested. "Someone probably shoved them off the platform, so they'd be inside the fence on their owner's property. It was just luck, I suppose, that the secret wasn't discovered then."

"Now can we live here, Mother?" Chris had stood it as long as he could. At the moment he had no interest in explanations, only in the gold at his feet—the gold and what it meant to him.

"Yes, Chris, we can. In fact, I'd just about decided to try it anyway. I've been thinking of turning this place into a small summer hotel. River House. It's too big for just the two of us in any case."

"Sounds just right to me. How about you, Chris?" asked Mr. Kenyon.

Chris nodded, his eyes shining.

"You'll have to give quite a lot of this to Uncle Sam, you know," Mr. Kenyon continued, "but if it's anything like as big as a haul as I suspect it is, you'll have quite a bit left over. And now——" He turned to Barry, his eyes twinkling. "I wish to state that I really am a writer. Not a secret agent or anything glamorous like that, I'm afraid. I read that famous piece in the paper and thought there could be a story in it. What I didn't expect was to get involved myself, even to the extent of being given a key to the gate and having to give assistance to young trespassers."

Barry and Alicia blushed.

"And did you find a story, Paul?" Barry's father asked.

"I sure did. Complete with two heroines, named Alicia and Barry. I think it'll be one of my best," he added. "If you girls don't mind, that is. Now, let's see how many goldbricks we've found, Chris."

Alicia edged over to Barry. "Imagine," she said, "Mr. Kenyon's going to put us in a book. Us! Gee, Barry, I'm so glad I came to live here in——"

"——in the whistle stop?"

"Yes! In this wonderful, exciting, marvelous whistle stop!"